ALSO BY CHRISTINA LI

Clues to the Universe

CHRISTINA LI

RUBY
LOST and FOUND

Quill Tree Books
An Imprint of HarperCollinsPublishers

Quill Tree Books is an imprint of HarperCollins Publishers.

Ruby Lost and Found
Copyright © 2023 by Christina Li
Library of Congress Control Number: 2023930013
ISBN 978-0-06-300893-9

Typography by Laura Mock
23 24 25 26 27 LBC 5 4 3 2 1

First Edition

To my family

RUBY
LOST and FOUND

ONE

YE-YE AND I had this rule: If you passed by a Chinese bakery on the way home, you had to make a stop. This was extra true if it was May's Bakery.

By this time last year, my grandfather and I knew by heart exactly which routes would lead to this off-chance, totally-by-coincidence-of-course encounter with May's Bakery on our walks back to his and my grandmother's apartment, right near San Francisco's Chinatown. Ye-Ye knew everything: hilltops to catch the sunset, parks where we'd spot old men doing tai chi on Saturday mornings, or stands where he could pick up surprise flowers for Nai-Nai.

When we did come across May's, we'd do the exact same thing. We'd stop and exchange a look. Ye-Ye would raise an eyebrow. "Egg tarts or coconut bread?"

And every time, I said, "Both?"

Dad, for some reason, didn't know to do this, even though Ye-Ye was his dad. Maybe the May's Bakery rule skipped a generation. This time on our way across the city to Ye-Ye and Nai-Nai's apartment, we passed by the storefront, with its bright red banner and yellow letters, and Dad didn't stop. He didn't even look back at me. It was probably because we were driving instead of walking, and Dad had to focus on traffic instead.

Dad cranked the NPR station up the louder the cars honked around us. I let down the window a little bit. The honks always made me anxious, but the breeze felt nice. A biker whizzed past, so close I could feel his jacket flap in my face. Dad started tapping his fingers on the steering wheel, a sign that he was getting impatient.

The light turned green, and we eased up and over the hill.

Mom turned around from the front seat to face me. She wore a suit jacket instead of her usual workout gear. She and Dad must have an important meeting today. "You got everything?"

I nodded. My phone was tucked into my pocket. My fingers gripped it tightly as if I were expecting a text any second, even though basically that never happened these days. My friend Naomi hadn't texted me in months, and my other friend Mia and I didn't talk as much as we used to. I ran through a mental checklist to make sure I wasn't missing anything. My clothes were packed in the duffel. I had my phone charger. My watercolor set was tucked some-where deep in there, in a big plastic bag, even though I wasn't quite sure why I brought it. I even had remembered to pack socks. The last time my family went on vacation to Yosemite, I'd forgotten to pack socks, and I'd spent the next two days turning them inside out and back again to wear before Mom finally was able to spot fancy hiking socks in the gift shop. But it wasn't going to be the end of the world if I'd forgotten my socks now. Home was just a drive away.

"Nai-Nai's excited to have you come," Mom said. "She even made you breakfast."

I mumbled, "I already ate breakfast." If half a Pop-Tart counted as breakfast. Which it did. For the record.

Mom sighed hard through her nose. It was her sign that she was getting impatient. The NPR radio host went on about how birds communicated with each other when they were migrating.

"This will be good for you," she said. I didn't answer. She glanced out the window. "Take this shortcut," she told Dad.

I knew that the shortcut wasn't going to be much faster, but at least fewer cars honked at us here. I'd actually gone up one of these streets, years ago with Ye-Ye, when we were looking for the tiger mural. I craned my neck to search for it again, but the stoplight changed and the car jolted forward.

I settled back and leaned my head against the window. If I came back to look for it again, I would have to do it by myself. Ye-Ye was gone. We pitched up another hill and then turned on to Bush Street, and soon the shops of Chinatown came into view.

Mom's tongue clicked. "That dumpling place just went out of business." She pointed at a sign. "I have to find a new place now." She poked her head out the window and glanced down the road. "Here, let's park in that garage."

Fifteen minutes later, I was standing in the living room of apartment 3B. Everything was still there—the couch with the tattered edge, the pictures on the wall. Ye-Ye's jade carving collection. The twin brush paintings that hung on either side of the doorway. This time, though, everything felt different. It was like I'd stepped into someone else's home.

My parents and Nai-Nai were in the kitchen, but for that moment I was alone in the living room. I picked up one of Ye-Ye's small carved lions, feeling the surprisingly heavy weight in my hand.

It would be so easy to slip out the door and down the stairs. I knew my way around this neighborhood. I knew where to get food and snacks. I knew where the bookshops were: the small one down the street, and the larger one a couple blocks away. I could go to the miniature brush-painting shop. It had been one of Ye-Ye's scavenger hunt stops, two years ago. I still remembered how to get there.

But I couldn't just run off. Running off was what got me in this whole situation.

"Ruby? Ruby-ah, where are you?"

I turned toward the sound of my name.

As I went to the kitchen and to my nai-nai, I told myself that I wouldn't run. Not now. Even if I knew every way home.

To be clear, neither Nai-Nai nor I had particularly decided that we should spend most of the summer together at her apartment. Mom and Dad made that call at the family meeting a few weeks ago. Dad sat there with a serious expression on his face, holding the detention slip that the school principal had sent them. Mom just sighed.

"Ai-yah, Ruby," she'd said. "You really had to end the school year on this."

I kept quiet. There was a loose thread at the bottom of my shirt. I yanked on it and unraveled a seam. The last time we'd called a family meeting, it had been to decide where to take my older sister Vivian out for a celebratory dinner after she got into her top-choice college. The time before that, Mom and Dad made me sit at the table with them because my reading and language arts teacher told them I was flunking my one-page homework summaries. I'd refused to read the assigned book, *Where the Red Fern Grows*, and instead was reading The Baby-Sitter's Club books in class under the desk. I'd told Mrs. Marconi that I didn't want to read the assigned book because I wasn't liking it, and someone spoiled it for me and told me that the puppies died at the end, anyway. Apparently my refusing to read about dying puppies was concerning enough for Mrs. Marconi to say something during parent-teacher conferences, which led to that family meeting. I read a few pages and got an A on my next homework. Mom and Dad were relieved. I then didn't do any of the later summaries and "forgot" to bring home all my other graded papers after that.

I couldn't really hide this detention from them, though, because the school secretary called both Mom and Dad about three seconds after I got assigned it. So now Mom and Dad were seated across from me. Viv was gone and off doing something with her friends, probably. I didn't blame her. There were infinitely cooler things to do as a graduated high school senior than watch your little sister get scolded at the dinner table.

"But *why* did you do it?" Mom asked it while she was rubbing her temples with her fingers, like I was giving her a headache and she was trying to physically massage it out. "Why do you always cause trouble like this?"

I yanked on the thread. All I did these days was cause problems.

Dad leaned back and crossed his arms. "Look, Ruby," he said, calmly, which is how I knew he was most mad. He liked to process information by sitting very still and swallowing it up. He would then set his jaw and talk. Quietly. "I know you're having a hard time. We're just trying to understand."

I didn't say anything. Mom took Dad aside and they had a hushed talk in the corner of the living room. I slipped upstairs. I'd hardly reached for my phone before I was called back down to the dinner table. By that point they'd decided that I would be spending every summer weekday at my grandmother's place. I'd stay there, too, Monday straight through to Friday, only coming home for the weekends. The whole summer.

After Mom and Dad left, it was just the two of us.

It wasn't like I hadn't been alone with my nai-nai before. I used to stay weekends when Mom and Dad were going away on a trip or when I just wanted to come over. When I was really little, Viv would come with me. Ye-Ye would go on walks or to do tai chi in the mornings after making me breakfast oatmeal with just a little bit of honey and mango in it, and it would just be me and Viv and Nai-Nai. She'd turn on the TV and busy herself with something, and the Mandarin would float in and out of my understanding. In the afternoons she'd take us to the fresh food market with her, and we'd follow her bright handmade flower pants through the crowd.

I knew every inch of this apartment. Nai-Nai used to say that I'd sometimes forget where the walls were because I kept running into them. One of the willow rocking chairs by the TV had a hole in the seat from when I was jumping on the chair and my foot went clean through. Ye-Ye put a pillow over it and told me not to tell Nai-Nai. Nai-Nai discovered it a few months later when she was dusting the chairs and she almost fell over herself laughing.

Now I nestled into the couch, feeling the springs under my butt. This apartment looked virtually the same from when I'd left it last, except now Ye-Ye was gone and neither Nai-Nai nor I wanted to be here together. I screwed my eyes shut. I tried not to think about what had happened in this apartment the last day I'd been here or what I could have done then.

I shifted over to a springless section of the couch, where the seat caved in just a little bit. I could hear Nai-Nai shuffling in the kitchen with her plastic slippers and the bubbling of the electric kettle. She couldn't quite look me in the eye yet. Maybe she blamed me for what had happened. She'd set me up with my room and then walked off. She didn't hum to herself or chuckle like she used to.

"Dinner, Ruby."

I rose from the couch. I could feel Nai-Nai's eyes on me.

I was being *watched*. Not just watched—grounded, because of my detention. And of all people, I was grounded with my grandmother.

"Why do I have to be with Nai-Nai all summer?" I'd asked two weeks ago at that family meeting.

Dad rubbed his forehead. "Well, you don't really have anything to do."

"And it's too late to sign you up for a camp," Mom said.

"We should have signed you up for soccer camp again. Or done robotics. Viv really liked that robotics camp."

"I don't like robotics. And I haven't played soccer in years."

"Okay." Mom looked at me, her lips pressed in a thin line. "Then you have nothing to do. So you'll go be with Nai-Nai. We can't—your dad and I need to go into the office. We can't watch you."

"You don't have to."

"I can't have you in this house alone. You're going to wander right off into the city."

"I wouldn't—" I slumped down. "That happened, like, twice. Besides, I'm thirteen. I'm too old to be watched."

"Not after what you did," Dad said, firmly, and I knew that it was final.

I'd stared out the window then. Mom was right about one thing: I didn't have a single thing to do. When I scrolled through Instagram, all I saw were stories of people going on road trips or hanging out by their friends' pool. I couldn't even get a text back from Naomi.

"Come on, Ruby-ah," Mom said. "Nai-Nai is lonely."

I turned to look at her. She knew I couldn't say anything to that.

We got dinner with Nai-Nai at a restaurant last week, after she'd returned from her friend Auntie Theresa's home in a beach town north of Los Angeles. Nai-Nai had left San Francisco back in February, less than a month after Ye-Ye passed away, and barely spoke to us all these months. Before, Nai-Nai would be talking nonstop about the weather or the prices of lychees or she'd be trying to match Viv up with her future husband based on her Chinese zodiac. But at the dinner, she stared quietly at her plate. Mom and Dad tried to talk to her. Viv attempted a few questions in Mandarin. I didn't even try. I stared at my kung pao chicken and stir-fried greens, and my stomach was in a big tight knot. Things weren't the same without Ye-Ye. I think we all wanted to talk about it but none of us wanted to bring it up.

"Please spend some time with her, Ruby," Dad said. "Just talk to her. You might help her feel better."

Now, sitting at the dinner table, Nai-Nai only looked up every once in a while from her bowl of ramen.

"Hái è-ma?"

Are you still hungry?

It was all she'd been asking me, every few minutes.

Are you full?

Are you still hungry?

Maybe it was all that she knew to say to me right now.

I sat with my bowl in front of me. "Bǎo-le," I said, with my rusty Mandarin. *I'm full.* I'd eaten all the noodles. I lifted the bowl and drank the soup, just so she wouldn't keep asking me.

"I'll make some oatmeal for breakfast tomorrow. And then we'll go to the senior center to meet up with some friends."

So that was how my summer was going to be. With my grandma and a bunch of old Chinese ladies.

Come on, Ruby. Nai-Nai is lonely.

Why did I have to be with her if she had the senior center?

I nodded. "Okay."

I got up and felt the soup sloshing around in my stomach. The silence stretched on between us. Maybe it was okay that we weren't speaking much, anyhow. Maybe that was how I liked it. For now.

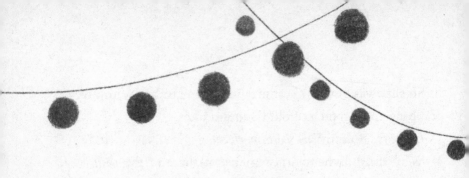

TWO

THE SENIOR RECREATION center was a couple blocks away from where Nai-Nai lived and smelled like linoleum and old oranges. Nai-Nai didn't complain when I slept until ten o'clock that morning, which secretly made me feel better. At home, Mom wouldn't let me sleep past nine before marching up the stairs and asking if I was sick. If there was anything the Chu family wasn't, it was late risers.

We walked through the doors of the senior center, and immediately I got the full attention of at least thirty grandparents. I gripped my mini backpack straps.

See, the one thing possibly scarier than being a new kid at school was being the new—and only—kid at a Chinese senior center.

"Evelyn!"

At the sound of my nai-nai's name, I turned. Someone

in a blue sweater rose from the edge of the far table, waving.

"May!" Nai-Nai steered us toward her.

She was exactly as I remembered. Nai-Nai used to always change up her clothes or her look, from flowery and bright to dark shades, from one lipstick color to another. She permed her hair one year and kept it straight the next. But May Wong always looked the same, pretty much. I'd see her around her bakery, and when she retired and handed the bakery operations over to her daughter, Annie, I always saw her in Ye-Ye and Nai-Nai's apartment, with her classic blue sweaters and her short, poufy graying hair, sipping tea. Or I'd spot her in one of the vegetable markets on a Friday afternoon, talking in rapid-fire Cantonese with someone over a pile of yams and making a lot of hand gestures. She talked to quite literally everyone—in Cantonese and English to Ye-Ye, in Mandarin to Nai-Nai, in English to my parents and me. She always gave me a hug when she saw me and always made me call her by her first name (May, never Auntie Wong or Wong Nai-Nai). She peered up at me from her tortoiseshell glasses. "Little Ruby, taller than me? Impossible."

She laughed and I couldn't help but smile. It was pretty easy to be taller than someone who was, on a generous day, not an inch over five feet in her sandal heels. "Hi, May."

"I remember the days your grandparents had to bring a step stool with you to the bakery just so you could see what was on shelves." May Wong paused. "Speaking of. I brought you something. Come sit. We're about to do crosswords."

As we walked over to her, I glanced around the long rectangular room. The walls were this off-white color, with sections of cracked paint. The tables were crammed together, so I had to squeeze by just to get to May. Playing cards were strewn across one end of a table. Crosswords and colored pencils lay across another. I sat on a rickety plastic chair right next to May, with Nai-Nai on the other side. Voices in Mandarin and Cantonese rose again as the others went back to their card games and conversations. May reached into her bag and pulled out something in a small white paper sleeve. "For you. I know these are your favorite."

I peered in.

"I hope you still like egg tarts," May Wong said.

I perked up. "Yeah. Of course."

"Some things don't change." May pushed her thermos near me. "Here, have some of my green tea with it." She leaned in and said, in a low voice, "Their tea here is awful." She opened the thermos bottle and popped in the button. She set the lid down and it doubled as a teacup, and then she handed me the hot cup of fragrant tea.

I let the tea warm my fingers. Nai-Nai asked, in Mandarin, "How'd the meeting with the landlord go, May?"

"Oh." May sighed. She responded, in Mandarin, "We're trying to negotiate it down. We're still going back and forth on whether to renew the bakery lease."

I looked up, feeling the steam dissipate from my cheeks. "Wait. What? What's going on with the bakery?"

May and Nai-Nai exchanged a look.

"It's nothing, child," May said. "Just rent going up a lot. These discussions happen every year." She nodded toward my egg tart. "Go on, eat."

I took a bite and savored the sweet, creamy egg custard, pressing down the inkling of worry in my chest. The crust was soft and flaky and melted on my tongue. "Thank you," I said, muffled, my mouth half-full. It was just like how I remembered it in May's Bakery on a busy Saturday morning or on a quiet Sunday afternoon, leaning over the counter to peer at the egg tarts and sponge cakes through the glass. I took a sip of the tea and leaned back, and felt warm and full.

That was, until Nai-Nai's other friend came later that morning.

"Did I miss doing crosswords?" she said, immediately upon setting down her tote bag. Over her pointy glasses, she peered at the sheets strewn around the table. "Good. That stuff bores me out of my mind."

Me, too. Except it wasn't just crosswords. This morning I found out the hard way that one of Nai-Nai's outlets didn't work. My phone sat like a brick in my pocket, out of charge.

Her fingers were clad with rings and her nails painted a

bright red, her short cropped hair streaked with gray. That was the first thing I noticed. The second thing I noticed was that she liked to purse her lips together. A lot. She looked quite a bit younger than Nai-Nai and quite a lot more irritated. Nai-Nai's friend pulled up a folding chair to the table, the legs clattering against the floor. She sneezed loudly into a handkerchief, and then groaned and said, in sharp-toned Mandarin, "Ai-yah, I can *feel* the dust in here."

"Hello to you, too," May Wong said mildly. "Someone's had a good morning."

"Well, I'm here now, aren't I?" the friend said. She leaned back in her chair. "Just in time for bingo. I'm ready to earn my keep and win my candy of the day." She looked up and finally fixed me with her gaze, and her eyebrows arched upward.

"This is Ruby," Nai-Nai said. "My granddaughter. She'll be with me for some of the summer."

"She'll be joining us," May Wong said, giving me a warm look. "And this is Auntie Lin, Ruby. She's been here the longest out of all of us. I've only been coming for a couple months."

"Ru-by," Auntie Lin said. Two hard syllables. I didn't like the way it sounded when she said it.

"That's me," I said. I put on a smile and tried, in my best Mandarin, "It's nice to meet you, Auntie Lin."

An eyebrow arched. "You speak pǔtōnghuà?"

"Yī-diǎn." *A little bit.* But the words sounded clumsy

in my mouth, like I was pushing around marbles. Still, she pursed her lips together into what kind of looked like a smile.

I relaxed. Maybe this summer wouldn't be too bad. It would just be me sitting here, watching them all play bingo, but at least they were okay with me around.

They passed out bingo cards and chips. And right before it started, Auntie Lin leaned back to speak to May Wong. She kept her voice low, but I was just close enough to hear her say, in Mandarin, "Another kid to babysit? What are we, a day care?"

May gave her a look. I felt my cheeks get all hot. They started calling numbers for the bingo game. Nai-Nai said something, but I couldn't hear. I looked up to see Auntie Lin staring at me. I glared right back and crossed my arms.

Guess what? I retorted, in my head. *It's not like I wanted to be here, either.*

I wished my phone was charged. Or I'd brought a book. Or even that watercolor set that I didn't think I'd use again, so I could do anything but this.

Also: *another* kid? Some other grandchild was being brought here against their will?

Five hours to go. The clock was literally slowing before my eyes.

THREE

"WELL?" DAD GLANCED over, his hands on the steering wheel. "How was your week at Nai-Nai's?"

I shrugged. "It was okay."

Five days and approximately seventy bingo games later, I was heading home for the weekend. Nai-Nai and I had gone to the senior center from Monday through Thursday. May was nice to me. Auntie Lin and I held mean staring contests. On Friday, Nai-Nai thankfully switched it up and took me to the market in the morning, where she bought vegetables and a big bag of lychees. I ate a couple of sweet, ripe lychees in the kitchen before retreating into my room. I scrolled Instagram with Nai-Nai's spotty Wi-Fi. People posted pictures of themselves kayaking in the bay and back-packing in the mountains. Mia had just posted a picture of herself posing on a lake dock, sunlight beaming down softly on her brown skin and curls. Naomi posted a series of pictures of herself at travel soccer camp, sweaty and grinning with her friends, her cheeks pink. Her new friends who were actually good at soccer, unlike me. I sighed and stuffed my phone under a pillow.

Dad came to pick me up a few hours later. I gave Nai-Nai an awkward hug to say goodbye, and then climbed into Dad's car, duffel and all.

"Ruby," Dad said. "Please give me more than that."

"I mean," I said, "there's not much for me to do at a senior center." I tuned most of it out. I sat next to Nai-Nai while they did crosswords. Or played cards. Or bingo. I played games on my phone until I heard Auntie Lin snarkily comment how teens these days are obsessed with their phones. After that I joined them for a round of rummy, just to make a point. I went back to my phone and played on it until the battery died. I had Viv's old hand-me-down phone so it had a battery life of like two hours. I spent the rest of the time counting the chipped ceiling tiles.

Nai-Nai also didn't do much after the days at the senior center. She used to always go on small trips and errands. Back when she was really into making clothes, she'd take me with her to the fabric store. We'd hang out for hours while she draped lengths of fabric over herself, so it looked like she had a rainbow cape. Or during her paint phase, she'd grab watercolors and have Ye-Ye and me paint with her. But now, like clockwork, we headed straight back to the apartment in the late afternoon. She wore gray sweater-vests and different varieties of handmade baggy pants. And her only hobby these days seemed to be watching TV.

"You could read a book," Dad said. He turned onto the road that dipped sharply down, so my stomach jumped a little. "There's a summer reading list going around, right? Or you could talk to your nai-nai. It would be a great time for you to . . . reconnect."

"Sure," I said. Dad knew the chatty Nai-Nai. The one who wouldn't stop talking about how the weather was affecting her joints or some piece of gossip she heard from May Wong. Mom called her luōsuo sometimes, which, in Mandarin, basically translated to someone who would talk your ear off. Viv called her loquacious. It was one of the fancy words from her vocabulary flash cards. I liked the way it sounded.

But this version of Nai-Nai still didn't speak at dinner. We sat by the window in the kitchen and ate. Nai-Nai cooked her egg-and-tomato dish, and she sometimes would cook too much rice for both of us. Then the next day she'd cook too little rice, and then to make up for it she'd cook too much rice, again. If Ye-Ye were here, he'd tell Nai-Nai, in his soft voice, about running into someone at the market and about the conversation they had. Nai-Nai would start a story a neighbor had told her, which would ramble on into ten other stories, and I would sit and listen to both of them, finishing each other's sentences. Now there wasn't really anything to fill the silence between us.

So I'd started watching TV with her after dinner instead of retreating to my room, because staring at my phone screen for a long time made my eyes hurt. Nai-Nai would cycle through the three Chinese dramas she was watching because she couldn't pick one. There was the old spy show, where everyone wore trench coats and ran through unlit streets. There was the historical one, where everyone wore long flowing robes. And then there was the modern drama about two movie stars who were friends as kids reuniting on the set of a movie they were filming together, which was the one I liked the best.

As the week went on, I found that I didn't mind watching the dramas with Nai-Nai, actually. We could sit on the couch and not have to say anything to each other. Plus, it was kind of nice hearing Mandarin again. I liked the way it sounded when Nai-Nai and the people on the TV spoke it, since Mom and Dad didn't speak it much. Mom and Dad were second-generation, which meant that Dad had grown up hearing Mandarin and Cantonese in Chinatown, and Mom had grown up in Seattle with her parents from Beijing, whom she still conversed with in Mandarin. But they didn't speak much of it to us because they said they spoke with an accent and had forgotten some words. They wondered if they should send us to Mandarin or Cantonese classes before they settled on Mandarin. And so Viv and I spoke it, but it always sounded all weird. Viv said it was like a sixty-year game of telephone between all of us.

Dad was quiet the rest of the way home. We turned onto our street. "Mom and I are grabbing coffee with an investor tomorrow. But Vivian should be coming home from her sleepover and around the house starting at ten, if you need someone."

I nodded. All Mom and Dad did these days was meet with people from companies with fancy names who supposedly had a lot of money to invest in their business. I didn't know much about their business, only that it had to do with energy. There was a lot of talk about the solar grid and something neutrality, whatever that meant. I used to hate that they were starting a business together, because it was the thing that got Mom and Dad to start fighting in the first place. After Dad got laid off and Mom quit her old job two years ago, they were really excited for a couple months at the start before they started arguing, first about their company, and then about everything. Where to eat. Where to take trips on the weekends. But things had gotten better over the last few months. Now they still had heated discussions about their work, but at least they didn't fight over dinner anymore.

"Viv doesn't have to watch me," I mumbled. I wasn't planning on doing anything tomorrow, anyway. I had texted Mia earlier today asking if she had time to call. I'd stared at my last conversation with Naomi and decided, for the hundredth time, that I wouldn't text her because I had nothing to say.

Dad sighed. "Sure. If you say so. And don't forget, your cousin Josh has a birthday party on Sunday."

"Right." I watched the orbs of the headlights on the wall expand as Dad pulled in. I pulled my duffel into the living room, where Viv was staring at her phone.

"Hey," she said, bounding up from the couch. One of her friends had just cut her hair so it fell around her shoulders. She looked up from her phone, and her long earrings jangled. "How's Nai-Nai?"

"She's okay."

"Cool." She shrugged on an oversize sweater from her high school. She turned to Dad. "I'm going over to Laura's, if that's okay." Without waiting for a response, she gathered up her tote and put on her shoes. The door closed, and Viv was out.

"Tiān-nah." I heard Mom sigh from behind me. She came out from the kitchen, wringing out a towel with her hands. She shook her thin hair out of her bun. "She's gone out every single day this week."

"Let her live, Katie," Dad said, going to meet Mom in the kitchen. He rubbed her shoulders. "It's the summer before she goes to college. She can do what she wants."

I dragged my duffel up the stairs. It thumped on every step.

Maybe there was a point when Mom and Dad would let me go wherever I wanted and do whatever I wanted. Viv no longer had to sneak out of the house or have her friends cover for her. Now she didn't have to reason with Mom or tiptoe around it with Dad. She could just go.

I had a feeling that for me, that was going to be many summers—and approximately three hundred more bingo games—away.

My FaceTime with Mia didn't go through at first. But moments later, my phone lit up with her contact picture and a FaceTime notification.

Mia Ortega-Anderson.

"Ruby-roo!" Mia said in her singsong voice, using her nickname for me. For a split second, happiness rushed through me and it was like old times again. "What's up?"

"Not much." I lay on my bed, holding the phone above me. "Well, actually, a lot has been happening. I really miss you."

"I miss you, too," Mia said, but she wasn't looking at me. Rays of sun streamed into the frame. "What's been going on?"

I sighed. Might as well come out and say it. "I, uh. Got grounded."

"Wait. What?" Mia's dark brown curls flew as she looked right back at me. "You? Grounded? But your parents never do that. So you have to stay in your house the whole summer? What happened?"

"Long story," I said. It had been almost a month since Mia and I last spoke. She was busy with her dance rehearsals, and then she told me she was on vacation with her family, and then she was having a sleepover trip with her friends. It all sounded amazing, but it was hard to feel happy for her when my summer seemed so empty by comparison. I still hadn't told her about what had happened with Naomi. I didn't want to. "My parents are overreacting, and they're making me stay with my nai-nai on the weekdays so she can watch me. I'm being *babysat*, Mia. It's awful."

"Aw, Ruby." Mia hugged her knees to her chest. "At least you get to hang out with your grandma. And you still get weekends to do stuff. Right?"

"Yeah." I didn't mention that Nai-Nai and I barely talked these days. Or that I did nothing on the weekends because I was grounded and couldn't hang out with anyone. I could practically feel Mia's pity from three thousand miles away. "How's New York?" I asked, switching subjects.

"Oh, my God, it's *hot*," Mia said. "And sticky. Especially in the subway stations. And it's humid. Like, the backs of my knees are sweating. I didn't know they could do that."

I laughed. "You didn't know the backs of your knees had sweat glands?"

"Did *you*?" She shifted her phone. "Even the cat has started lying next to the fridge all the time." She turned. "Hello, Simburton."

The orange cat raised his head, blinked once, yawned, and lay back down.

"Where's Charlie?" Mia also had a King Charles spaniel. I loved both.

"On a walk with Mom. Anyway," Mia said. The phone frame shook, so I knew she was walking through her apartment. Soon, I saw the lavender walls of her room and the corners of her music posters. "Yeah. It's *hot* out here. Going to dance these days is miserable." She drew her hair up and wrestled it into a bun. "But I got to go with Ingrid to her family's lake house in Vermont last week. It was nice and cool there."

"Oh, right. I saw your post." I heard about Ingrid all the time. She shared a homeroom and dance studio with Mia.

"Isn't their lake house *awesome*? They taught Anika and me how to Jet Ski and kayak and stuff. We got really good at kayaking."

"Anika," I said, slowly. "Dance friend?"

"Homeroom. She sat across from Ingrid in Madame's class. We made a group chat to complain about the French homework and then we kind of became a squad."

I felt queasy. Mia was talking about her new friends so easily, as if she knew them her whole life. As if she forgot about the weekend before she moved away because her dad found an even better professor job in New York, when we slept over at Naomi's house and Mia cried until one in the morning and said that she would never find friends like us again.

"Naomi hasn't texted me in months," I blurted out without thinking.

Mia's smile dropped.

The instant I said it, I wished I hadn't.

"Aw, Ruby. I'm sorry," she said softly. She shifted uncomfortably. "Why? What happened?"

"Nothing," I said quickly. Even if it was mostly a lie.

"Really?" Mia's brow furrowed. "That doesn't sound like Naomi. I . . . could text her for you?"

"No," I said. I felt bad for bringing it up. "That's okay."

We were silent for a long moment. Mia looked down at the floor.

Way to go, Ruby.

We used to FaceTime for hours, back when Mia first moved to New York at the end of last summer and couldn't stand the thought of living there. She'd narrate her entire day to me. She'd describe the pigeons on the street and the noisy subways. She'd talk about how hard private school was and how everyone had all their friend groups already and how she didn't like wearing a uniform. She talked about hating how cold the winters were and how she was trying to convince her dad to let her live with her grandparents in San Francisco so she could come back to my school. We talked until her screen got dark because she was three hours ahead and it was supposed to be her bedtime but she was FaceTiming me from under her covers. She could talk about anything for hours while I listened. That's the way it had been since second grade, anyway.

But now we'd already run out of things to say. And the calls were getting shorter and shorter.

"I have to go," Mia said, finally. "I have rehearsal. We can call some other time?"

"Okay." I swallowed. "Have fun."

Mia dropped off the call. I shifted and my phone slipped out of my hands, hitting me in the nose. "Ow," I said to no one.

All last year, there had been a small awful part of me that felt glad whenever Mia complained about New York, because it meant there was a chance that maybe she would hate it so much that she would come back to San Francisco. And then maybe Mia, Naomi, and me would be right back where we were.

But now there was a new Ruby and a new Naomi in Mia's life. Mia was settling into New York. Liking it, even. And she was staying there for good.

After my FaceTime with Mia ended, I lay on the bed for a while, just kind of staring up at my ceiling. It was dotted with glow-in-the-dark stars that Ye-Ye had given me for my eighth birthday. But over time, the Big Dipper had become the handleless spoon, and the stars had lost their glow.

I rolled over and began taking my dirty clothes out of my duffel to put in my laundry hamper. My fingers jammed into something hard at the bottom, and I pulled out the watercolor set.

I was never going to use it. I sighed, and then reached over to put it in my nightstand drawer. It held a bunch of things that I got tired of over the years but never really wanted to throw away, like sticker books or fun erasers. I opened the drawer and dropped the watercolor set in there. It landed on an old map, crunching the paper. I reached out to smooth the corner of the map down, and then I pulled it out to refold it.

It was a worn map of San Francisco, on the verge of tearing, that Ye-Ye always carried on the scavenger hunts. It accidentally ended up in my small backpack after last year's scavenger hunt. I was supposed to return it to him, but I never did.

Ye-Ye made me a scavenger hunt every August, the weekend before school started. There were colored-pencil marks over all of this map, a different color for every year. Dark green was last year. Gold was the year before, then red. The last time that Viv joined us for the scavenger hunts was recorded in a beautiful sky blue, looping near the ocean. Viv always liked to charge ahead with each clue, as if it was a race to finish as fast as possible. I liked to wander. And then the next year she stopped coming.

I crouched over, retracing the lines with my finger.

Ye-Ye loved collecting maps everywhere. The map of

Paris reminded him of the sun. The map of Nai-Nai's family hometown in China had a lake in the center, so it looked like an eye peeking out at you. Ye-Ye said that San Francisco once looked like a giant thumb, jutting out into the water like that. "You live on the left part of the thumb," he said to me, pointing to where Mom and Dad and Viv and I lived. "And Nai-Nai and I live on the right part of the thumb."

Over the years, Ye-Ye had doodled on this map, and the routes unfurled like colorful threads. He drew seals by the beach and clouds around the bay. He put smiley faces over my house and over his and Nai-Nai's apartment, and drew a path between them. And he put a big star over the spot where May's Bakery was.

Looking at the map for too long made my chest hurt. I didn't want to think about what this year's scavenger hunt could have been. Carefully, I folded the map back up, taking extra care to lay down the creases. I slipped the map into the drawer and closed it shut.

Last August, Scavenger Hunt Stop 1

Start from home sweet home.

I clutched the small piece of paper in my hand and met Ye-Ye's smiling eyes. I knew immediately where we would head, even without the help of this first clue. And that the scavenger hunt wouldn't begin at my house.

Sweet home.

"We're starting from May's."

Ye-Ye laughed. With his soft voice, he said, "What gave it away?"

"This is where the scavenger hunt begins every year, Ye-Ye." I grinned. "Of course I know."

The scavenger hunt would obviously start from the bakery. The heart of the city for both of us. Plus, there was no better way to prepare for a day of walking up and down the hilly sidewalks than eating all the sweet and savory treats you could.

The map with its colored pencil markings stayed folded in my little backpack as I hopped down the stairs and out the front door of the apartment complex. Above us, Ye-Ye's neighbor Mr. Leong leaned out of his window to water his plants and waved down to us. We waved back. "Nei-houma?" Ye-Ye called up, in Cantonese. Mr. Leong grinned. "Gei hou-ah!"

I didn't need the map to get to May's. The route was

straightforward: we'd walk down three blocks, past the church and then the small park. I tried to not walk so fast, because my legs had gotten longer and Ye-Ye was getting older these days. We'd turn left, and before long, we'd be standing before a small bakery with a big yellow and red banner, crammed in between a produce market and a Chinese pharmacy. I stood transfixed on the street, my stomach rumbling and my eyes glued to the char siu buns and the sesame balls and coconut bread in the window display. I heard May's voice coming from within, calling out orders. It was as if I was five again, grabbing on to Ye-Ye's hand as he led me to the familiar bright red sign, where the warm aroma of toasted coconut and sweet cakes wafted out the door, and we promised every time we passed by here, we would stop in.

Now we paused in front of May's and we didn't even have to say a word to each other before we walked in.

May's hadn't changed a bit over the years. The brush painting of a peony was on the far wall, and the Chinese calendar was tacked on right next to it. Sometimes when the sun set, the light came in exactly so the rays would touch the flower painting, turning the petals to a pale peach color. The fan roared in the corner. I stared longingly at the shelves in front of me, which were filled with egg tarts, pineapple buns, sponge cakes glistening with sugar glaze, and deep-fried dough fritters. The last one used to be Viv's favorite. She could eat five of those things on our scavenger hunts. But now it was just Ye-Ye and me.

"Ruby!" May Wong peered over the shelves. "Both of you are here so early!"

"Hi, May," I said.

Ye-Ye walked up to the counter. "Today's scavenger hunt day," he said.

May's eyes grew wide. She pushed her glasses up. "Wah!" She leaned over and looked at Ye-Ye. "Where are you going today?"

"I haven't a clue," Ye-Ye said, and we all laughed. It was a bit every year between the two of them. Ye-Ye had laid out the locations and devised the clues each year. "Ruby will find out."

"So you will," May said. "Well? Are you excited?"

I grinned. A nervous thrill fluttered in my chest. A whole day exploring the city and egg tarts for breakfast. Nothing could be better. I looked up and said, "Of course."

FOUR

I HAD YET to successfully get out of my cousin Josh's birthday parties.

My aunt and uncle lived at the north end of San Francisco and sent Josh to a private school, so I never really saw him around except for when they hosted parties. Every year, without fail, during Christmas, birthdays, and Lunar New Year, they decked out the house and Mom and Dad pulled me and Viv along to see them.

Who *had* two birthday parties, anyway? Josh already had a big climbing gym birthday party with his friends. But his parents insisted on inviting us all over for dinner. My consolation this year was that Viv couldn't get out of it, either. Usually, she was busy at some camp or doing her summer job. But this summer she didn't have anything to do. She fiddled with her jean jacket and put her phone away as Mom knocked on our aunt's door.

"Ruby, you've grown!" Aunt Tiffany gushed at me as she opened the door. Mom's younger sister was three inches shorter than her and even louder. She moved down here from Seattle seven years ago with her family, which is how I came to know—and forever be compared to—my perfect cousin Josh. Now my aunt herded us in. A mountain of shoes had already piled up. Voices poured in from the kitchen. As was the case in every Asian party I went to, I didn't recognize half of them.

"Ah, you're here!" Uncle Andy was in the kitchen, filling a plate with potstickers. "I'm so glad the whole family could make it."

Dad peeked around the corner. "Happy birthday, kid." He clapped Josh on the back. Dad loved goofing off with him. "Thirteen? Big year."

Josh grinned broadly. "Thanks." He had this confident smile that everyone loved. Kid modeling agencies, his soccer coach, his teachers.

"New hair?"

"He insisted on the cut," Uncle Andy said, shaking his head. "He says that's what all his friends are doing now."

Dad shrugged. "Looks better than I did at twelve. I still had a bowl cut then. Can you imagine? My ma really put a bowl upside down on my head and cut around it. Everyone avoided me at my middle school dances."

Josh laughed with him.

Aunt Tiffany turned to my sister. "And wah, Viv, now you're all grown up and headed to college! I saw your *beautiful* graduation pictures." She held her at arm's length. "Carnegie Mellon engineering, right?" Viv nodded. "Well, they're so lucky to have you. Going across the country, too!"

Mom and Dad beamed. "Vivian couldn't get rid of us fast enough," Dad said, with a small bit of a smile.

Aunt Tiffany squeezed Viv's hand. "How are you feeling?"

Viv grinned. "I'm pretty excited."

"Wonderful," Aunt Tiffany said. "We hope Josh grows up to be like you someday. Don't we, Josh? I'm already hearing such wonderful things from his teachers. He's in all the accelerated programs. That should give him good chances for an honors track in high school."

Blegh.

They barely looked at me. I was used to it. Every family party was like this—the parents circled around with compliments that sounded more like backhanded brags. Aunt Tiffany once said that she wished Josh was more relaxed like me. I'd never seen Mom so red in the face.

When I wasn't put in the accelerated math program in sixth grade, Mom and Dad tried to play it off, but I could hear them talking about it behind closed doors. Dad insisted on watching me do my math homework at the kitchen table, and I could see him wilt a little as I pulled my crumpled sheets out of my backpack. "You need to organize, Ruby," he said quietly. He stared at me. "And focus." I tried telling him that everything my math teacher said always went in one ear and out the other, or that I had a hard time paying attention, but Dad just called them excuses. And, like with tardiness, the Chu family had no place for excuses.

But all that didn't matter right now. Everyone's attention was on Viv and that's how I liked it. Now that I'd acquired some powers of invisibility, I tried to sneak a potsticker off a plate.

"Ruby, lǐ-mào," Mom said, slipping into Mandarin to scold me. *Manners*.

I jerked my hand back.

"Go ahead," Aunt Tiffany said. "Kids get hungry." She turned back to my parents. "Oh, by the way, the Zhous are over here. I think you met at our last Lunar New Year party?"

As Aunt Tiffany steered my parents toward the voices, Josh pulled a potsticker off the plate and popped it into his mouth.

"Happy birthday," I said.

He glanced at me, his mouth full, chewing for a sec. Then he nodded. "Thanks, Ruby. What's up?"

I shrugged. "Not much," I said. Josh pulled his phone out of his pocket. "You?"

He looked up from staring at his screen. "Hmm?"

"Never mind."

"Wanna play Xbox?" Josh said to Viv and me.

"Sure," Viv said. Josh flipped on the TV and turned to battle games. I knew that Josh would get overcompetitive and shout things at the TV. Viv and him liked to compete. I just liked to button mash and see what happened. That was how it always was. When we were younger, Josh would throw a fit and quit Monopoly games if he wasn't winning. Now I watched him hunch over his controller. Still, this was better than the alternative, which was to sit at the adult table and listen.

We heard, anyway.

"So how's that company of yours going?" Aunt Tiffany asked.

"Great, actually," Dad said. "We're in our funding phase right now and trying to meet with investors. We're working around the clock, I mean, but it's stuff that we're really excited about."

"Seems like it," Uncle Andy said. "I mean, it's like a light's on in your eyes."

"A lot of late nights." Mom sighed. "But worth it."

"What an inventive bunch," Aunt Tiffany said. "Like father, like daughter, right?"

I knew which daughter they were talking about.

"Oh, this one's light-years ahead of me. I wouldn't be surprised if our companies are competing in a few years," Dad said, and laughter roared from the table.

The tips of Viv's ears were pink, and she stared hard at the screen.

"Hey, Eddie, what's up?" Josh got a FaceTime. "Sorry, can't hang out right now. I'm with my cousins. Tomorrow, though?"

"What about Ruby?" Aunt Tiffany said. "How's she been doing?"

Mom's voice dropped low, and my stomach sank with it. What was there to say? My bad grades, or how I landed in the principal's office for ditching school at lunchtime and got detention? "Ruby, she's . . . well. Trying."

Aunt Tiffany's tongue clicked. "Middle school is always hard," she said. Josh glanced over at me. I wanted to tug the strings of my hoodie and shrivel up within my own sweatshirt. "Besides, last year must have been hard for her, with your father and all." She turned to Dad. "How are you doing?"

"Holding up," Dad said. "We all miss him in our own ways. But I think it really hit Ruby."

Silence. I knew what Dad was implying. I was the only one who couldn't *hold up*.

Mom said, "She's having a hard time."

"She'll be all right," Uncle Andy said, breaking the silence. "The kids always figure things out. Some may take a little bit longer to figure things out, that's all."

I squeezed my eyes shut. My character lost their third life. Viv and Josh were still battling it out. I gave up on playing.

"Of course," Mom said.

"And she has a great sister to look up to," Aunt Tiffany said.

Viv glanced sidewise at me. She'd heard the whole conversation. Everyone had. I stared ahead. At this point, invisibility didn't seem like a bad idea at all.

We were finally able to leave my cousin Josh's birthday party after nearly an hour of the guests all trying to say goodbye to each other. Mom and Dad came out of the party laughing, but they quieted down once Dad started driving us home.

"Well," Dad said, meeting our eyes in the mirror. "How was your cousin reunion?"

Viv shrugged. "It was nice. We played Super Smash Bros."

"What about you, Ruby?" Mom said. "Why weren't you playing much with them?"

"Because I didn't feel like it."

The corner of Mom's smile turned down, and instantly I felt bad for ruining the mood. Dad inched up the hill. "I think you should talk to Josh more," she said. "I know you two go to different schools, but you could hang out with him sometimes. He's a good example."

"I'm *grounded*," I said pointedly. I really would rather be grounded than hang out with my smug cousin. "Remember?"

Mom frowned. "I don't appreciate this tone, Ruby."

I wanted to tell her that I didn't appreciate overhearing her tell everyone and their aunties that I was *having a hard time*, but I didn't say that.

"Come on," Dad said. He looked over at Mom. "Katie. We don't need to push it."

From the back seat I could see her cross her arms and look out the window, away from me and Dad. Viv gave me a sorry look and then went back on her phone, her thumbs flying at the speed of light.

We pulled into the garage and headed into the house in silence. Mom turned to Dad. "Did you get those forms signed and scanned over to Owen?"

Dad asked, "What forms?"

There was a pause. "The contract," Mom said, exasperated. "I can't believe you didn't—"

"I'm going to Steph's place," Viv announced brightly.

Mom turned halfway. "Really? It's late."

"It's okay," Viv said. She jingled the keys that Dad had set down on the kitchen counter. "I'll drive."

"Fine," Mom said. "Just go."

Thirty seconds in the house. That must be a record. I watched my older sister breeze out the door she'd entered just a minute ago. Mom kept arguing with Dad. I trudged upstairs and closed the door to my bedroom.

At least if my parents were arguing with each other, they couldn't focus on me. But that didn't make me feel much better, not at all. I sat on my bed and scrolled through my phone. If it were last fall, I would be texting Naomi all the annoying things about Josh because she knew him from travel soccer, and she'd tell me a funny story about him and how obnoxious he was on the field. We'd text for hours, because Naomi liked to send a lot of texts in a row with a lot of exclamation marks. But even if I texted her now, she probably wouldn't respond.

My plan to bring a book to the senior center on Monday and tune everyone out fell apart from the moment Nai-Nai and I walked through the doors. For starters, there were two more people at May Wong and Auntie Lin's table. They looked up and I stopped in my tracks.

The good news? I was no longer the only kid at the senior center. The not-so-good news? I recognized him.

"Ruby!"

What was *Liam Yeung* doing here? He still wore his polo shirt and cargo shorts. His hair was still unruly.

"This is wild!" He flashed his grin with one dimple and my heart sank.

"Oh," I said. "Hey." Maybe if I kept it to one-word greetings, I could sit in the corner and we could just go about our separate—

"You two know each other?" May Wong jumped in.

I dropped my backpack on the seat next to Nai-Nai and sat down. "Yeah," I said. "We, uh, go to the same school."

"And same grade," Liam jumped in proudly. "*And* the same

class, for two weeks before before I got moved to another homeroom. We were project buddies in social studies." He turned to the person who I assumed was his grandmother, sitting in the chair right next to May Wong. He said something to her in Cantonese and turned back to me. "Ruby, this is my maa-maa."

She was his paternal grandmother, then. Like his version of Nai-Nai. That much Cantonese I knew. She had straight, short white hair that was parted down the middle. She was bundled up in an oversize knitted sweater, with a bag of yarn and knitting needles in her lap. "Nei-hou," I said. "Sorry, I don't speak a lot of Cantonese."

She grinned. She and Liam had the same toothy smile, except she had dimples on both cheeks. "Good thing I know pǔtōnghuà, too," she said in Mandarin, and winked at me.

"Hǎo-ah, Ruby," Nai-Nai said, settling into her chair. She was in a good mood. Today she wore her handmade flower pants and a collared shirt. She even spent a few minutes in the morning putting on lipstick. She almost forgot her sweater before we left, and I had to remind her. And now she was practically elated with relief. "That's great. Now you have a friend."

Finally, I could almost hear her add. I gave her a strained smile.

"Well, this is all cute," Auntie Lin said coolly, flicking a piece of lint off her sweater. "You kids can go bother each other now."

I bristled. Why did she always have to sound so dismissive of us? "Yeah, you don't have to babysit us anymore," I said sarcastically.

She shot me a glare and then glanced around the table. "Anybody in for a round of cards?"

I scooted out of the circle and off to the side, letting the chair grate against the floor so it annoyed Auntie Lin.

"This is actually very cool," Liam said, oblivious, as he plopped down on the chair right next to me. "I thought I'd be the only kid here. Now it's like a club or something."

"Two people can't make up a club," I said.

"Well, I'm sure we can recruit someone's grandkid somewhere," he said, looking around. He hoisted a laptop bag up to the table and it made a thump. It was so big that I was sure it contained government secrets or something. People stared at him a lot when he first came to school in March because he was a) a new kid, b) who moved in the middle of March, wearing c) a faded Teenage Mutant Ninja Turtles shirt and a weird lumpy knit sweater and holding that massive laptop bag. But he didn't open it now. Instead he kept asking questions. "We haven't been here for a few weeks. When'd you start coming?"

"Right when school ended." *Please don't ask why.*

"Why?"

"Because."

"'Cause why?"

"Because I felt like it." Maybe I should just tell Liam.

After all, he probably knew the reason why better than anyone else. He was there in the principal's office that day when I was. I turned to him. "Why are *you* here?"

He shrugged. "Because I want to."

I couldn't tell if he was joking or not. "Really? Why aren't you, like, doing normal things with your summer?"

"Like what?"

"Like . . . I don't know. Hanging out with friends?"

For a second I wondered if I had gone too far. But Liam wasn't fazed. "Okay," he said cheerfully. "Well, why aren't *you* hanging out with friends, then?"

I opened my mouth and then closed it very quickly because I had nothing to say.

"Sorry," Liam said. "That was mean of me."

I laughed. Liam's comment should have stung but it didn't. It was kind of hilarious, actually, in a sad way. We were two friendless weirdos hanging out in a senior center. "That's okay. I asked first."

"Do you actually like coming here, though? I don't see you here much."

"Not at all," I said. "Do *you*?"

"I mean, yeah?" He shrugged. "I like coming with my maa-maa. We started hanging out here during spring break. Everyone's always nice to me."

He really wasn't joking.

"And they all have the wildest stories." He nudged his head toward the corner of the room, where a group of men

45

were playing cards, their voices rising above one another. "You know Mr. Tung over there? He used to be a fighter pilot and still has, like, near-perfect eyesight. And Mr. Ding is a brush painter. He gave my maa-maa a painting to hang up in our new apartment, 'cause right now the walls are still kind of bare and there aren't many decorations. And Auntie Moy used to act in all the TV shows."

"Hmm." I glanced over. That grandma had snow-white hair that was gathered into a perfect bun. I could kind of see it, actually.

"I haven't talked much to your grandma, though. She's newer here."

"Yeah," I said. "May Wong brought her here. She was away before."

"Ooh, really? Away where?"

I shot him a look. This was just like in social studies, when he had like fifteen questions about Mesopotamia and somehow got into a whole discussion with Ms. Wellington about the history of grain. (Who talked about the history of grain? And when did this kid ever run out of questions?) I glanced over at his laptop bag and changed the subject. "What do you do on that?"

"Oh, this?" Liam tugged out his computer and it made a loud whir as he booted it up. "It's my computer. I like to play games. Wanna see?"

I paused. "I'm good," I said. I reached into my backpack and pulled out my book. I'd taken it from the apartment that morning, and I brushed dust off the cover.

"Ooh, a book," Liam said, peering at the cover. "What's . . . *The Phantom Tollbooth* about?"

"We'll find out." I glanced over. "Weren't you going to go play games?"

"Oh. Yeah, okay. I get it. I'll let you read." His computer whined.

I turned back to my book with its worn pages and the creased spine. I didn't tell him that this wasn't my first time reading the book. That, in fact, I had read the book over and over again last year before I gave it to Ye-Ye to borrow. And that in the world before that Saturday morning, he'd meant to give it back to me.

Last August, Scavenger Hunt Stop 2

In the little house that hides on green,
make a trade and stay awhile.

"What *kind* of house is it?"

Ye-Ye shrugged. "It's all in the instructions."

"Yeah, but what *kind* of a little house is it?"

And then we played a bit of twenty questions.

"Is it the size of a bread loaf?"

"Slightly bigger."

"Is it the size of my room?"

"Much smaller."

"Is it a dollhouse?"

"No, but size wise, you're onto something."

After a while, I deduced that this very-small-but-not-Wonder-Bread-small house was somewhere on Green Street, because Ye-Ye got all smiley when I made that guess and he wouldn't include any words that weren't parts of the clues. So we walked up and down Green Street. We passed the brunch spot that Mom and Dad liked to take us on special occasions and the Philz Coffee that Viv liked to hang out at with her friends. It was fruitless.

"I don't see anything."

"There's more to the clue, Ruby," Ye-Ye said. "Think. A little house that *hides* on green."

I looked to the end of the street. "Hides." I thought for

a moment. "Hides. *Hyde* Street?"

His eyes lit up. I'd gotten it.

I ran to the end of the street and waited for the Walk sign. I crossed the cable car lines and there it was.

"Is *this* it?"

The Little Free Library was a blue cottage with a small thatched roof and painted flowers blooming on the walls. I leaned closer, and I could even make out a small painted rooster on the side. A door was fastened with a little knob. *A little house on green.*

I looked back and Ye-Ye was grinning.

"I found this on my walk the other day," he said. "It wasn't there before. They must have built it up in the past year. So I wanted to show you."

I reached out and pulled on the doorknob and peered in. Books were scattered about the two shelves.

"See any book you like?"

I scanned the shelves. *French Cooking with Julia Child. How to Invest in Real Estate. The Phantom Tollbooth.*

The last book was fraying slightly at the spine, so I could just make out the title. I peered in and gingerly took it out. I remembered the book was on some summer reading list.

I began to put it back. "Wait," Ye-Ye said. "Keep it."

"But I don't have a book to replace it with."

"Well," Ye-Ye said. "Luckily, I do." He showed me. *A Guide to Hiking in Northern California.*

I looked up.

He shrugged. "It's not like I'll be going hiking very much anymore. Your ye-ye's knees aren't quite what they used to be." He took a Post-it out of his pocket and wrote on it before sticking it to the inside flap of the book.

"What'd you write in it?"

"Oh." Ye-Ye showed me the inside of the front cover. *Property of Raymond Chu.* Except he crossed out his name and wrote next to it, on the Post-it, *To the next wonderful stranger who decides to pick this book up. Happy trails.*

We poked around the library a little bit more and then walked away from there, *The Phantom Tollbooth* tucked in my backpack. Weeks later, I would visit Ye-Ye in the study of his apartment and tell him about Milo and the watchdog named Tock who always thought time was running out and how there was a witch named Which and a bee called the Spelling Bee. I would tell him about the adventures Milo had and how he encountered these islands called Conclusions that they had to jump to and how they ate cookies in the shape of the alphabet. It was a strange book, and when I told Naomi and Mia about it, they raised their eyebrows and went, *Huh.* But it was my strange book and for once, I didn't really care.

Ye-Ye asked to borrow it from me and I gave it to him. He loved it, maybe even more than I did. And all the while, his book on hiking sat tucked away in the Little Free Library, sheltered from the fog and wind and rain.

FIVE

"WHERE DID I put the sugar?"

Nai-Nai shuffled around the kitchen. I chewed on a toasted s'more Pop-Tart. The good thing about being at Nai-Nai's was that she kind of let me eat whatever I wanted. She wouldn't get mad at me because I ate things that didn't have all five food groups in it, like Mom would.

"You put the sugar in the cabinet," I said, without looking up.

"Hmm," Nai-Nai said. "I usually put my spices there. The sugar is on the counter."

I sighed and crammed the rest of the Pop-Tart in my mouth and went over to the cabinets. I opened the top one. Sure enough, the jar of sugar was there.

"Oh, thank you, Ruby," Nai-Nai said. "I don't even remember putting it there."

This wasn't the first time it had happened. The other day, she left the package of tofu out on the counter after cooking noodles. When Nai-Nai came for breakfast, she stared at the tofu package and asked me why I'd taken it out for breakfast. Nai-Nai was always a bit scatterbrained. She often left mail and receipts out on the coffee table and left books she was reading open and facedown. But she never really misplaced things in the kitchen.

Now Nai-Nai spooned sugar into her oatmeal. We ate in silence. After breakfast, Nai-Nai gathered up her bag and tugged on a sweater over her pink dress. I put on my backpack. She fussed over her hair a little and we were out. Nai-Nai glanced at the shops on the way and pointed out a bouquet of hydrangeas. "You think these would look good in the apartment?"

I shrugged. "Don't know."

"They *are* pretty."

"Cool," I said curtly.

Nai-Nai sighed. We continued our walk to the senior center. Auntie Lin was sitting at the table when we got there.

"Morning," Nai-Nai said. "How are you?"

"Spent the morning arguing with the cats," Auntie Lin said in a bored voice, looking up from the crossword. "They think that just because I'm old and senile means they can trick me into feeding them two breakfasts."

Nai-Nai laughed. "They deserve an extra treat every once in a while."

May Wong came in next. "I'm so sorry I'm late," she said. She set her bag down. "I was talking to Annie about the bakery."

"Everything all right?" Nai-Nai asked. "How's that going?"

"They're just . . . we're going back and forth. Rent's still going up. Developers keep approaching us with offers that are hard to turn down. Especially since you know the bakery's barely earning a profit in the last couple years." She glanced at me and smiled wearily. "Morning, Ruby."

"Hi, May." I looked at her curiously. This wasn't the first time she'd brought this up. "Wait, what's happening? Why are developers approaching you?"

"They . . ." May waved a hand. "It's a long story. But developers have been buying up places in Chinatown for a while. And they're looking at the bakery."

Panic struck me. "Wait—they're not—the bakery's—?"

"Don't worry, Ruby," May said smoothly. She didn't quite meet my eyes. "The bakery will be fine. We'll figure it out. It's just a lot of hard conversations, that's all." She looked around. "Is it time for crosswords?"

The door swung open as Liam came in, holding the door for his grandmother. They came over to our table. Everything I'd just heard about May's Bakery took a back seat in my mind as I saw Liam. Now I had to spend the morning putting up with the bright-eyed chatterbox who never quit.

Liam flashed his one-dimpled smile. "Good morning, aunties." He helped his grandmother into a chair. She and May greeted each other in Cantonese. She then pulled a thermos out of her bag and her current knitting project, which looked like the beginnings of a sleeve. Huh. Now I knew where Liam's lumpy sweaters had come from.

Even Auntie Lin softened around him. "Morning, kid."

Please don't come sit near me please don't—

"Hey, Ruby."

"Hey." I looked up.

"How's the tollbooth?"

"The what?"

He pointed at my book.

"Oh. Good."

"Really?" His eyes lit up. "I saw it at the library yesterday. Maybe I'll check it out. We could start a book club."

"You should," I mumbled. I didn't have the heart to tell him that, again, things with two people weren't really clubs.

I met Nai-Nai's eyes. She nodded toward Liam and raised an eyebrow. She wanted me to become friends with him. It couldn't be more obvious. But what could we talk about?

How was the rest of your seventh grade?

Pretty good. How was yours?

Oh, you know, got detention for two weeks. Like you saw that day.

I turned my chair away from Nai-Nai and crossed my arms. Liam asked a million questions a minute. And I had a feeling that if I smiled back, if I tried to talk, if anything, he might bring it up, and I just might have to explain what happened.

Liam and I were both in the school office that day, although for different reasons. The new kid from Oregon happened to get bonked in the nose playing knockout in gym class at around the exact same time the vice principal spotted me trying to sneak back into school after lunch. So while Liam was waiting to see the nurse, trying to stanch the flow of his profusely bleeding nose with his Teenage Mutant Ninja Turtles T-shirt, I was passing him on the way to see the principal for ditching school.

I wasn't even ditching in the cool way like they did in those high school movies, where they went to race cars or something. All I wanted was to get lunch. And walk around. But instead I ended up in the principal's office. The secretary placed two calls, one to Mom and one to Dad. When they *both* showed up to pick me up from school that day, I knew I had really, truly gotten into trouble.

At that following family meeting, when Mom and Dad both asked me, over and over, why I'd done it, I didn't answer because I couldn't bring myself to tell them that I started ditching because it was better than sitting alone in the lunchroom.

Even if it was kind of the truth.

It didn't start out like this. After Mia moved the summer before seventh grade, Naomi and I still sat together at lunch. It sure wasn't the same without Mia. Before, she'd always wait for us at the lockers. "You *have* to hear what happened in gym today," she'd say, tucking her curls behind her ears. Naomi and I would follow her to the lunchroom. "They had us play kickball, and I was chosen last, as usual. And then I thought I would bunt when they pitched to me but then—" She laughed into her hands. "I literally. Tripped over. The kickball."

"Oh, my *God*, Mia," Naomi said, but she was smiling.

"I really wish you were there," Mia said. "You could have played for me. Scored a homer."

And then she'd launch into another story. Naomi would offer me her fruit and I'd swap it for my fruit snacks.

Naomi and I didn't quite know what to talk about without Mia. She would still swap her cantaloupe slices for my fruit snacks. Her parents were always trying one new healthy food thing or another and wouldn't let her have anything high in sugar. She told me about her family's annual Big Sur camping trip. When she got a new phone, finally, she showed me, in its clear glittery case. "They're not letting me have my phone during dinner," she said. "And they won't let me call people after midnight, either."

She blew her light brown bangs out of her face. She'd had bangs all the time I knew her, but now they were at the length where they were too long to be bangs, but too short to be tucked behind the ears. "Being an only child sucks sometimes. I feel like I'm watched like all the time."

At least they're paying attention, I thought. Mom and Dad didn't go two days without starting one of their "discussions," which would get louder until they were arguing from different floors of the house, their voices echoing like some awful surround sound movie. Or they were fretting over Viv, who was applying to colleges and occasionally sneaking out of the house to see her friends. I told all of this to Naomi, who drank her oat milk. "That's not cool. But at least they're leaving you alone."

A group of girls walked into the lunchroom then, and Naomi brightened. "Oh, wait," she said. "I have to tell you. I just made the travel soccer team!"

"That's amazing!" I hugged her. "I knew you'd crush it at tryouts."

"I was kind of scared, because the forwards are, like, really good. But I made it! Coach Craig said I had a lot of potential, as long as I keep up the drills."

One of the girls in the group spotted Naomi across the lunchroom. She waved at Naomi and motioned for her to come. Naomi hesitated, and then shrugged, as if to say, *Sorry, I'm with her.*

Another girl from the group glanced over at us. "Emily

Hunter's the star of the team. She's *really* good. She also kind of scares me."

"Yeah, I bet." Emily was in social studies with Naomi and me. She was the kind of person who had a stare that made you self-conscious. Like you had spinach between your teeth or something.

Naomi and I sat at the same table all the way through winter break. When Ye-Ye passed away at the end of January, she was the first to show up at my house with cookies and a hug. At lunchtime, she sat across from me and kept asking if I was okay. I guess she didn't know what else to do. We ate in silence a lot. I wished that Mia were here across from me. She would know what to say. We Face-Timed, and she sent me a really long email about how sorry she was and how good of a person Ye-Ye was, but she wasn't here.

Then things started to change.

Our class seats got switched up every month. At the end of March after spring break, Em and Naomi got seated next to each other in class. I saw Em lean over to whisper something to Naomi while they introduced the new kid Liam to the front of the class, and Naomi giggled. Another day they walked in with matching hair ties. And each day, Naomi looked longingly toward the table where they all sat during lunch.

"Trade?" I held out my fruit snacks.

Naomi said nothing.

"Hellooo?"

She looked back at me. "What?"

The next day, when our big social studies civilizations project was being announced, Ms. Wellington told us to pick our partners. I turned toward Naomi, but she and Em had already turned toward each other. I tried to turn toward someone else, but everyone had already paired up. Except for Liam.

"Ruby, you'll be with Liam," Ms. Wellington said. Em stared. Naomi looked away. We'd talked at lunch about how weird Liam seemed. He grinned from across the room and waved. I gave a tepid smile.

I went up to her after class. I made sure Liam was out of earshot when I asked, "Ms. Wellington, can I . . . work on this alone?"

"Ruby, it's a partner project," she said. She gave me an encouraging smile. "I'm sure Liam will be a great partner."

I dragged my feet to lunch. By the time I'd arrived, our usual spot was empty. And then I looked toward the table, where Naomi and her travel soccer teammates were talking and laughing over something.

Naomi caught my eye, and then looked away quickly. My heart sank into my stomach. I sat down at our usual spot and ate my fruit snacks, each of them sticking to the roof of my mouth.

After school, I walked right up to her at the bus stop. "Seriously?"

Naomi looked at me from under the hood of her raincoat. "What?"

"You ditched me in social studies! And at lunch!"

"Well, Em asked me first," she said. "I couldn't say no to her. And also you weren't at lunch and they invited me. So I went."

"I was *late!*"

"You could always join us," she said, even though she didn't sound like she meant it.

"No thanks," I said. Spending lunchtime being stared down by Em did *not* sound fun. "You've been friends with these people for like two weeks, and you're already doing everything with them?"

"For the record, they're actually really cool," Naomi said. "And I play with them all the time."

"That doesn't mean you have to *attach* yourself to them," I said sourly.

She straightened up. "Are you, like, jealous or something?"

Jealous? "I'm not." I stepped back, swiping rain from my cheeks. "You're just being kind of an awful friend right now. What about me? What about Mia?"

"Mia is in *New York*," Naomi said. "And last I checked, we're allowed to make new friends as well. Which I'm sure Mia is doing, since she seems to be moving on just fine." She set her jaw. "You could, too."

I stepped back. Naomi must have seen the hurt in my

expression, because she pressed her palms to her eyes. "Look, I know this year sucks for you, okay? Like, I'm really sorry about . . . everything . . . that happened to you and your family. But I can't just be *your* friend all the time."

The bus chugged out exhaust, and I snapped my eyes shut. "Then don't."

I felt bad, but only hours later. I tried sending Naomi a text but I chickened out.

We didn't sit together again. Before, I was always sad that lunch was only thirty-five minutes. Now it seemed to drag on forever. Being alone in a cafeteria wasn't the worst thing. It was being alone in a cafeteria across from someone who used to be one of your best friends. I sat by myself at my old spot for a week before taking my lunch into the library. I ate my turkey sandwich between the bookshelves. I memorized the last names of the authors that started with a *B*. The librarian pretended not to notice, until on a Wednesday in May, she told me that the superintendent had walked through the library and told her that they couldn't have anyone eating in there.

I was slowly trudging back to the cafeteria when I saw it.

Someone usually sat in front of the exit doors near the science rooms, but that day, the chair was empty.

And before I could even think much, I pushed through the doors, and I slipped out. The door clicked closed behind me.

Wait.

How was I going to get back in?

I panicked for three seconds before remembering that we always got let out for fifteen minutes of recess after lunch. I could always come back when everyone was at recess and be let back in.

Now I could do whatever I wanted.

I walked around to the entrance and slipped between the bushes. I walked down the block until I realized there was a park around the corner. I sat down on one of the benches under a tree near the swing set, and I ate every bite of my lunch. I watched the birds and remembered when Ye-Ye and I would watch the pigeons while playing Weiqi at the park near his place. I slipped right through the bushes and waited for one of the monitors to look the other way before joining the four square line. All this time, my heart beat quickly and a kind of a thrill picked up in the pit of my stomach, like I was in the car with Dad going down one of those steep hills.

I knew I couldn't do it every day. But occasionally, I could slip out and enjoy lunch at that park. I brought a little bit of my allowance so I could buy a small ice cream sandwich at the shop on the way home. Once, when I made it back too late for recess, I walked through the front door. "My mom just dropped me off," I lied, my palms sweating. "I wasn't feeling too well."

They barely looked at me before they waved me through.

I should have stopped then. But I didn't. The next time

I was trying to slip back into recess, the vice principal was waiting for me by the doors. She looked me in the eye, chewing her gum. "Ruby? Principal Merrill would like to see you in her office."

That was when they told me that the vice principal had seen me leaving the school.

And that was the moment I was given detention.

And that was what led to this summer.

Me. Here. Being babysat by a bunch of grandmothers.

I was sitting on Nai-Nai's couch that night and watching one of the three Chinese dramas she was keeping up with when my phone buzzed in my pocket.

I pulled it out to see new texts from—

Naomi???

hey!! the first message said.

I sat straight up on the couch.

i know we haven't talked in a while and things have been kinda weird between us

but

i miss you a lot!!! and we've always spent my birthday together and so i was wondering if you would still be down to come over to my house next thursday night for a sleepover? :)

My heart raced.

Naomi didn't just text me. She *quadruple-texted* me.

I frantically scrolled up to the last text I sent her.

Did I *do* something? Did something change for her?

Maybe she realized that she was wrong for dropping me as a friend. Ye-Ye always said that things happened when you were looking the other way. So this was it. Maybe Naomi just wanted to talk to me again because she missed me, and we would stay up all night talking and FaceTiming Mia. Things would be normal again. Or as normal as they could be.

My thumbs flew over the screen as I typed back. **you still have extra sleeping bags, right?**

I sent the text and threw my phone down on the couch. I looked around. Nai-Nai was shuffling around in the kitchen. And then I picked my phone back up again, because I couldn't help it.

The three dot bubble.

The three dot bubble!!

yeah!!! :) and also my mom is making way too much carrot cake as always so pls pls come

I was about to text back when I realized that I was still very much grounded. I wasn't supposed to hang out with anyone for a whole month after school ended. And a sleepover was definitely 100 percent off limits.

I leaned back. I *had* to go. I never missed Naomi's birthday.

I glanced toward the kitchen, where Nai-Nai was. An idea began to dawn on me.

I mean, it *was* during a Thursday. And maybe during the week, Mom and Dad's rules didn't count. Because I was at

Nai-Nai's. I'd be back by Friday morning.

And my parents wouldn't let me sleep over, but Nai-Nai just might. She wouldn't know the rule about not seeing friends, would she?

I texted back. **ofc i'll be there. can't wait :)**

I just had to hope that it would all work out.

!! see uuuuu :)

I rose up on the couch, hugging my phone to my chest. I silently fist pumped and jumped so high on the couch that I practically put a hole through that, too.

I just had to convince Nai-Nai.

SIX

THE DAYS DRAGGED on. I texted Mia to FaceTime Thursday morning while Nai-Nai and I made breakfast. She was talkative. She asked me three times if the room was too cold. "I feel like it's especially foggy these days," she said, closing all the windows. She watered the plants around her sink. She glanced at me when I sneezed. "Don't forget to bring a sweater, too, Ruby. Are you wearing socks at night?"

"No. Why?"

"Ai-yah," she said, shaking her head. "You should wear socks at night, or you're going to catch a cold and your knee joints will get all stiff."

"Okay."

"And you'll develop arthritis."

"Okay."

"And then I'll have to make you those bitter herbs from the pharmacy."

I sighed. I knew I wasn't going to get out of this.

"Hmm," she said. "Maybe I should brew a chicken broth for you next week."

I shrugged.

Nai-Nai held my gaze for a moment. She pressed her lips together. She opened her mouth, as if to say something. And then she sighed. "Okay. Let's go."

Before we left, I checked discreetly to make sure she was carrying everything in her tote—her sweater, her heart medicine and her wallet, her phone, and a backup deck of cards just in case. Nai-Nai was the first one to arrive that morning. May Wong came shortly after, seeming distracted. And then Liam came with his grandmother and he held the door open for Auntie Lin. I dragged my chair off to the side, and, like clockwork, Liam plopped next to me.

"Hey, hey, hey, Ruby."

I kept my eyes on my book. "What's up?"

"The sky."

I looked up. "Really."

"It's a joke."

"A prehistoric one."

"Nothing wrong with prehistoric jokes. You think that dinosaurs asked each other what was up?"

"Probably when the asteroid came around."

Liam's eyebrows shot up, his mouth in a perfect circle. And then he doubled over, laughing so hard that even his grandmother flashed us a clueless, toothy grin, her knitting needles clacking. "*Way* too soon," he said, straightening up. "Nice one, though."

"Here all day."

"Anyway," Liam said, swinging his laptop onto the table. He reached into his bright green drawstring bag. "I brought two controllers today. Just in case you wanted to play some Rocket League with me."

"What's Rocket League?"

"It's like soccer, except it's with cars instead of soccer players. You wanna give it a try?"

He booted up his computer and it whined to life.

"Um," I said. "I'm good."

"It's fun. You should try at least."

"I'm not really a gamer."

"You don't have to be. It's really easy to learn."

I looked at the loading screen, and then I glanced back down at my book. "I'm still good."

He shrugged and plugged in one of his controllers.

"Okay, hear me out," Auntie Lin said from the table. "I'm getting bored of rummy. What if we played a more exciting game? Like poker?"

"Not this again," May Wong said.

Liam's grandmother put her knitting needles away and

said something in Cantonese. Everyone laughed, including Liam.

"What's she saying?" I whispered.

"Oh, she's asking if Auntie Lin wants them to gamble away their pensions."

I chuckled. Liam looked sidewise at me and I snapped back to the book. He put his headphones on. I was at the section where Milo met the watchdog, Tock. While I was reading, I kept sneaking glances at Liam's computer screen, which was lit up with bright colors as the cars zoomed around. Liam concentrated on the screen, the tip of his tongue sticking out the corner of his mouth.

It looked kind of fun, actually. I turned back to my book and smoothed down another page.

On the walk home from the senior center I got a text from Mia saying that she was too busy to FaceTime tonight. She sent another text saying that she was probably free on Saturday, but I knew when Saturday rolled around, something else would come up. It was the third time she said she was too busy and that we could call later. At this point it probably wasn't going to happen anymore.

I sighed through puffed cheeks and put my phone back in the pocket of my hoodie. Nai-Nai looked over.

"Zěn-me le, Ruby?" *What happened?* "Is everything all right?"

I nodded without saying anything.

"Really?"

I nodded again. We climbed the steps to apartment 3B and walked in.

"You know," Nai-Nai said. "Yeung Nai-Nai's grandson Liam is trying to be friends with you. He brought a thing for you to play games with him. That's nice of him."

I looked up. "I know."

"It's just Liam and his ba and his nai-nai, you know. They said they moved here so the nai-nai would feel more comfortable in a Chinese American community."

I wondered why it was his dad and his nai-nai. Maybe his parents were separated. Maybe his parents had fought, just like mine did. But still, I didn't know what to say.

"It's hard for the kid to move around so much, though. Apparently it's the third time he's moved in three years. According to his nai-nai it's been three months and they still haven't put away their boxes yet."

"Okay."

Nai-Nai turned to me. "Ruby, what I'm trying to say is, that kid needs friends his own age. And I think he wants to be friends with you."

"I *know*, Nai-Nai." But we didn't even talk at school. What was I supposed to do now?

I stalled until Nai-Nai sighed and gave up the subject. "Are you hungry? I can make an early dinner."

I shook my head. "Not hungry."

"How about some tea?"

"I'm *fine*, all right? I'm not hungry or thirsty or whatever all the time." All I wanted was to listen to some music and try to make myself feel better about the whole Mia thing. I turned to go to my room.

Nai-Nai set her bag down. "Child, what on *earth* is going on?"

I stopped in my tracks.

Nai-Nai's expression hardened. "I've been trying to figure it out for days. What is happening with you?"

I opened my mouth and then realized I didn't know what to say.

She charged on. "I've tried making you good food. I've tried asking you questions. I thought it was a bad week. But this is all you're like now." She took a deep breath, her eyes flashing. Ye-Ye said when Nai-Nai was angry, it was like a sunstorm because it was always for a few minutes at most and then she'd be calm again. But she didn't back down. "I know this summer is not the best for you. But I just need you to tell me. What is wrong?"

My breaths came quickly. "What's *wrong*?" A lump rose in my throat. "I'm *here*, okay?" I could see the hurt in Nai-Nai's expression, but I couldn't stop now. "My mom and dad don't even want me around in the house because I'm such a messed-up kid and all I do is create trouble."

"Ruby-ah," Nai-Nai said softly. "Why do you think that?"

"Well, I'm stuck with you, aren't I? Everyone else is having fun over the summer and I spend all day at the *senior center*. For old people."

Nai-Nai put a hand on her hip, her expression deepening into a frown. "You don't think I wish you were with your friends every single day? I don't *want* you to have to be stuck at the senior center with us. I don't know what your parents were thinking. You think I want to be worried about you all the time? May asks me every day how to make you feel better while you're sulking in the corner and I just know she feels awful about it."

The mention of May deflated me. I didn't want to hurt her. I didn't want to hurt anyone, but it seemed like I couldn't help but do just that these days. "I'm not—*sulking.*"

"That's all you do!"

I crossed my arms. "Fine. I won't sulk."

"That's not it." Nai-Nai's voice faltered. "Ruby-ah, you didn't used to be like this."

Her words sunk in.

"I—" Now my throat was so tight it was hurting.

"What? What now?"

I balled up my fists so I wouldn't cry. "I *can't* go back to that anymore. That—the old Ruby. You know I can't."

Nai-Nai said, her voice soft, "What do you mean?"

My voice broke. "Not after Ye-Ye."

I finally said it between us. Nai-Nai looked at me, her expression wilting, and it broke my heart.

I pushed the words out. "It's like everything kept going after he passed and I just stopped. And everyone just seems to move on and move away okay but I *can't*, and I'm *trying*, but I'm just—stuck. By myself. And I can't talk to anyone about it."

"You can talk to me."

"But I couldn't. Not for these past months."

Nai-Nai met my eyes, and she knew. We were finally going to talk about it.

I looked down at the table. "Why did you go?"

Nai-Nai was quiet. I couldn't swallow back my words.

"You didn't talk to us for that whole month after the funeral," I said, and now my voice was rising, too. "Mom and Dad weren't talking about it, either. And Viv just stayed in her room all day. And I came over by myself because I thought I could—talk to you, or something, and—you were *gone*. Without telling anybody. We were all worried sick."

"Ruby-ah," she said softly.

I hurtled on. "And when Theresa ā-yí finally called us and told us you were at her house, I asked her if you could come back. But she said that you needed to stay for a bit, with her, and that you'd be back soon. But you *lied*. You were gone for months and months. We thought you didn't want to see us anymore. I thought—I thought that you forgot about Ye-Ye. I thought that you didn't like us anymore."

She flinched. "Why would you ever think that?"

"That's what people do when they don't like their families," I said. "That's what I always read in books. They run away."

"Is that true?" This time, Nai-Nai sounded sad. I felt awful. I'd probably said something wrong again. But it was all out there. It was like puking when you had the flu. I felt horrible, but at least I didn't feel sick anymore.

"I woke up the morning after the funeral," Nai-Nai said. She clasped her hands together. "And I felt like I couldn't do anything. I felt like I couldn't move. I got up and made breakfast and went downstairs for a walk like I always did. Sàn-sàn-bù. Because that always made me feel better."

She sighed. "But then I started walking and walking. I made it to the end of the street before I realized that this was the path that I walked with him in the mornings. And somehow I couldn't walk another step. So I went home. I tried it the next morning. I got out of bed again and I walked to the end of the street and I stopped. I realized that . . . that I couldn't go anywhere, because everywhere reminded me of him."

"Ye-Ye?"

"Yes. Ye-Ye." Nai-Nai looked down at her hands. "So I stayed in the apartment, and I sat in this chair, and I just sat and sat, and the longer I sat, the sadder I got. I felt like the walls were closing in on me, Ruby. I don't know how much time had passed, but I remember calling Theresa and telling her that I needed to come down for a week, maybe, because I couldn't get around my own home. And then she drove up."

"And then you went to stay with her."

"She said the sun would be good." Nai-Nai reached across the table. She took my hand. "And it was. Theresa lived by the sea. Each day I would go down to the water and look at the sea and think about Ye-Ye. But I didn't mean to leave you. Or our family. I thought of you every day, Ruby. I always meant to come back. It just . . . took me longer than I thought it would."

Nai-Nai's hands felt soft and tough and wrinkly all at once. Her palms were warm, and her grip was strong. I thought of how much you must love someone that you can't bear to be at home once they're gone. Suddenly emotion was flooding me and I wanted to say everything to Nai-Nai but the words couldn't come through. So I pushed myself up from the table. I didn't want Nai-Nai to see me like this. "I have to go get something," I mumbled, not looking at her. "I'll be right back." And then I went to the room that was mine for the summer and I sat at the foot of my bed and I curled myself into a little tight ball.

I stayed in that room for a long time, my head between my knees.

Nai-Nai hadn't abandoned us, I realized. She was just hurting far more than we knew.

Finally, I stood up and knew something had changed.

I walked out into the living room. Nai-Nai was watching one of the three Chinese dramas, the one about the two movie stars.

She looked up at me when I walked in and paused the episode she was watching.

"I'm sorry," I said. "For saying that you ran away."

I didn't know how to say sorry for everything else. For not talking to her. For ignoring her when she spoke. But I thought it, and I thought it as hard as I could and hoped she heard somehow.

"Well," Nai-Nai said gently. "I'm glad I'm back."

I settled on the couch next to her. Nai-Nai reached to turn the TV off.

"Wait," I said. "Let's keep watching."

"Okay," Nai-Nai said. She started playing the episode again. I turned to watch, snuggling against Nai-Nai's crochet blanket that she made.

This time it was quiet, but for the first time it wasn't the kind of quiet that made me feel like I had to say something to fill it. We'd already said it all.

I pointed at the screen. "They really should have just talked things out with each other before they starred in the movie together," I said.

Nai-Nai laughed, the first real laugh I'd heard from her in a while. "If only they were as smart as you, child."

I leaned back. Finally, the silence was peaceful. Nai-Nai and I were watching TV, curled up in her blankets. The crickets hummed outside. And then my stomach let out a loud rumble.

"Are you hungry?"

I covered myself with the blanket. "Not really."

Nai-Nai gave me a look.

"We just started!"

"Ai-yah, the show can wait, can't it?" She glanced at the screen. "It's recorded, anyway. Come on. I'm making you tofu-noodle soup. May's supposed to stop by later. I'll make her some, too."

I nodded and peeled myself from the crochet blanket to go to the kitchen. And Nai-Nai got the pot and the noodles from beside the stovetop, and I went through the spice cabinets to pull out all the spices for her. White pepper. Five spices. I searched high and low before I found the black pepper next to the sugar. And while Nai-Nai heated up the beef broth I made a mental note to put them in the places they were supposed to be when I was done, so Nai-Nai wouldn't misplace them again.

After dinner we settled back down on the couch to watch TV. I pulled the crochet blanket around me and Nai-Nai had just started another episode when there was a knock on our door.

"May's early," Nai-Nai said, pushing herself up from the couch. "Maybe she'll watch with us."

She opened the door and May walked in.

"May? Just in time! Watch some TV with us?"

May Wong wrapped her sweater around her, heaving a deep sigh.

"What's wrong?"

May didn't say anything. She just sank into the couch and looked ahead, listlessly. Nai-Nai and I looked at each other.

When May finally looked up at us, she said, "I just came from talking to Annie and the developers. We'll have to sell the bakery."

SEVEN

NAI-NAI AND I didn't speak much that following Monday morning on the way to the senior center.

"She can't be losing the bakery, can she?" I blurted out last Thursday night after May left, while Nai-Nai was washing the green beans in the sink. "People love it there. They're always coming and going. Business can't be bad."

"May's is popular," Nai-Nai said, sighing. "But it's still not easy for businesses here to make profitable margins." She shook out her hands, spraying droplets of water. "She's had these worries in the past. I know she talked to your ye-ye about it sometimes. She's always sorted it out, some-how."

"So the bakery will get through it," I said, leaning on the now-wet counter. "Right?"

"I don't know." Nai-Nai sighed. She turned the tap off.

"The bakery can only chēng-dé-zhù for so long."

I knew that phrase. It meant to strain under the weight of something immeasurably heavy. It didn't make me feel any better.

I stayed up late that night, curled up in my bed. I could hear Nai-Nai snoring through the wall from the other room. I couldn't stop thinking. To distract myself, I scrolled through YouTube videos in the dark. I watched a video on what would happen if the Earth were shaped like a doughnut. I typed a text to Mia asking her when she was free. I deleted it before I pressed send and watched the words disappear from my screen. What would we talk about, besides me throwing all my worries at her?

I spent the weekend in my room while Mom and Dad and Viv bustled in and out. I sat there numbly that next Monday morning while Nai-Nai and Auntie Lin hovered on either side of May, trying to comfort her. Well, Nai-Nai hovered. Auntie Lin just kind of sat there, lips pursed. According to Auntie Lin, Liam's dad was taking his grandmother for a doctor's checkup, and so Liam wasn't here, either. I was secretly glad. I knew he would ask a billion questions about the bakery, and I didn't want to hear them. The rest of us—Nai-Nai and Auntie Lin and I—knew just how dire this was.

"They kept raising the price of the space at a ridiculous rate," May Wong explained to everyone, echoing what Nai-Nai had said. May had been too upset to talk much at Nai-Nai's place and had stayed home Friday, so she was only now explaining the situation to everyone. She clasped her hands around her thermos. She looked like she always did, with her hair neatly in a clip and the same tortoiseshell glasses. But now, there were worry lines around her eyes. "They've been doing this forever. First they raised the rent in the seventies. We barely got through that. The roast duck shop next to us folded in the nineties, but we kept going. But it didn't get easier and we're barely staying afloat and . . ." She put her face in her hands. "I talked to my daughter Annie. I doubt we can make it this time."

Auntie Lin, for once, didn't say anything snippy. "Is there something we can do?"

May Wong shrugged. "Not much, my friend. Unless you could keep this city itself from raising rents, which isn't likely. Annie and I are talking about how to get around it. We've scheduled meetings with our landlord and with some local community advocacy groups to discuss our options."

"You'll find a way," Nai-Nai said. "I'm sure of it."

I didn't say much. I couldn't imagine May's Bakery not existing. Ye-Ye was gone. There would never be a scavenger hunt again. We couldn't lose the bakery, too.

May caught my eye. I must have looked awfully worried, because she gave me a reassuring smile. Even in her distress, she was looking out for me. If anyone could get through this, it was May. She would figure out a way.

Nai-Nai said she always did. And that made me feel just a bit better.

Nai-Nai and I kept watching TV at night. When we weren't talking about May and her bakery, we were narrowing down from watching three Chinese dramas to just the one about movie stars who used to be childhood friends and who were now reunited and falling in love on set. At this point, we watched more than one episode a day. And I was getting better at understanding Mandarin.

"There are *sixty* episodes to this thing?" I said one day after I googled the show on my phone. I sank into the couch. "How could this go on for *so* long?"

"Typical Chinese drama," Nai-Nai said. "Remember, there aren't seasons. They just make one long complete story."

"This thing could be ten episodes if it had to," I said. "Also, she shouldn't be dating her other costar. That's going to cause a lot of trouble. Plus, he's going to break her heart. He's an awful person."

"Oh, sure," Nai-Nai said. "But it's telling each other their true feelings that's the hard part. Plus, you have to include all the good stuff. We haven't gotten an airport running scene yet."

"The classic." I pulled the blanket around me. "Crushes seem very complicated."

Nai-Nai laughed. "They are rather inconvenient. Liking

your ye-ye made me move across this whole country."

"Oh, right. Ye-Ye said you grew up near New York City."

"And I would have stayed there my whole life, too, if it weren't for his stubborn self."

Nai-Nai and I were talking. We weren't used to talking without Ye-Ye around, but somehow, in the past week, we'd begun to learn. She was starting to crack jokes and I was laughing at them. I learned that she liked tea first thing in the morning, scalding hot, so I began the electric kettle in the morning if I woke up before her. By now, we'd pretty much set a routine. We'd eat breakfast and then go to the senior recreation center, Monday to Thursday. Nowadays before we left, Nai-Nai would do her hair and lipstick. Auntie Lin came three days a week. Liam and his grandmother came most days. May Wong came every day except Friday. Sometimes, we'd swing by the store after we left the senior center to buy some flowers, because Nai-Nai liked the way they looked. And then we'd come peek at the mail—

My head snapped up. Mail. That was what we forgot today.

I rolled off of the couch. "I'm getting the mail," I said over my shoulder. I grabbed the keys from the hook next to the door and headed down the stairs. I reached Nai-Nai's mailbox and the key clicked. I grabbed the envelopes and took the stairs by two back up to Nai-Nai's place.

"There's a letter from——" I squinted at the return address. The envelope felt a little heavier than normal. "Theresa. Oh. I think it's Auntie Theresa."

"It must be the pictures." I handed the envelope over to Nai-Nai, who slowly tore the front flap. She leaned back with a contented sigh. "Oh. These are the butterfly pictures."

"Butterfly pictures?"

"From near where she lives. In Pismo Beach. Every year, the butterflies migrate there for the winter."

I looked over at the printed photo. There was Nai-Nai standing in a forest, bundled up in a puffy coat and a scarf. Her permed hair was blown to the side. She was looking over her right shoulder.

"Your ye-ye and I have been wanting to take a trip down to somewhere like Pismo for years," she said. "He always said he was going to stop by during the butterfly season. And when I was down there, I didn't know if I wanted to go, because I didn't want to see them alone. But she convinced me, and we drove down for that day."

We turned to another picture, with a close-up on Nai-Nai's face. Her cheeks were red, her expression lit up with a smile, her eyes filled with wonder. A butterfly perched on her shoulder, its wings folded.

"You got one!"

"I had to be very, very still. I didn't even know one had landed on me." She paused, and then pointed. "I look happy here." She said quietly, "I didn't know if it was wrong to feel happy so soon after your ye-ye passed."

I gave her arm a squeeze. "I think he would have loved seeing you get happy over butterflies."

"Maybe," Nai-Nai said, softly. She leaned back. "Sara ā-yí was so good to me, you know. She really took care of me during that time."

"Sara?"

Nai-Nai looked at me, confused. "Who is Sara?"

"You mean Theresa?"

"Yes. Theresa ā-yí. Who is Sara?"

"You said—" I closed my mouth. "Never mind."

We pored through the pictures. There was one where Nai-Nai's hands were outstretched, the monarch butterfly beyond her reach. "We can go next year. They'll be in the same place."

"It's actually programmed in their genes," I said. "I learned that during Ye-Ye's scavenger hunt two years ago. They always know where to go when they migrate south. But they don't live for very long, so sometimes it's only their kids that come back."

"But they always do come back," Nai-Nai said softly.

"And they know exactly where to go home," I said. "Isn't that cool?"

"Yes," Nai-Nai said. And as the rays of the setting sun filtered through the window, the light turned her cheeks golden. "It is."

* * *

Two years ago, Ye-Ye and I stood in the butterfly exhibit of the California Academy of Sciences. It was hot and muggy in the glass dome. The museum docent told us that they wanted to keep conditions as similar as they would be in a rain forest.

Ye-Ye and I leaned over the railing and watched him feed a butterfly that was a bright, brilliant blue. The guy laid out a bottle cap and the butterfly hovered over it for a moment before softly landing on the edge.

"What do you feed the butterflies?" Ye-Ye asked.

"Mostly water with a bit of sugar in it," the guy said. "Sometimes I'll give them fruit juice or Gatorade."

I perked up. "*Gatorade*? Really?"

"Oh, yeah," the guy said. "Every once in a while. The butterflies love that stuff."

I used to drink Gatorades all the time after soccer practice. I imagined the butterflies in their hot rain forest, drinking some Cool Blue. The thought made me smile.

"Do these butterflies just live in the rain forest?" I asked, bending low enough so it was like I was making eye contact with the butterfly itself.

"These ones do," the guy said. "That's why we have to keep it humid so it's like what their homes would be. You wouldn't see these around the streets of California, that's for sure. It's mostly the monarchs around Santa Cruz, when they migrate down for the winter."

"They always go to Santa Cruz?"

"They come down from up north and spread around a couple places here in California," he said. He gently tapped the sugar-water-Gatorade-soaked cap, and the butterfly took off. "Some near San Luis Obispo, too. They always know to return to the same places for the winter."

"How do they know?"

"It's fascinating, actually," the guy said. "They always know where to fly to, and they always know where to fly back to."

"Oh," Ye-Ye said faintly. "I read a book about that last year, actually. From a poet I really like."

I looked at the guide. "Do they ever get lost?"

"Not really. Very rarely."

"So it's like they have a built-in map."

"Yes, exactly. It's like it's programmed into their DNA. And they're excellent pollinators along the way, because they travel such long distances. Would you like to see the *Heliconius sara*?"

"You seemed to be really interested in that butterfly exhibit," Ye-Ye said as we left the rain forest room. The air seemed especially cold, and I didn't realize how humid it was in that exhibit until I unstuck my shirt from my back and wiped the sweat from my upper lip.

"We talked about pollinators in science class," I said. "Mr. Martinez talked about butterflies and bees and how they helped plants grow. My friends and I did a whole class project on it."

"Really?"

"Yeah, we did a presentation on them," I said. Me and Mia and Naomi. "Naomi watched a documentary with her family about it. And set up a whole fundraiser at our school to raise money to donate to a conservation fund. Did you know that without pollinators, the world would literally end?"

"Really."

"Yeah," I said. "Because butterflies and bees help pollinate everything and help plants grow."

"Sounds like it was a fun project," Ye-Ye said.

"It was." I didn't tell him about how I spent hours looking up YouTube videos and how I went down a Wikipedia rabbit hole. I wiped some more sweat from my forehead. "I'm hungry. Can we get some lunch?"

"Let's eat," Ye-Ye said. "And you can tell me more about this. You know, one day you could fill a museum exhibit of your own."

"Maybe," I said, doubtfully. But Ye-Ye glanced over at me, and he didn't have the faraway distracted look that Mom and Dad had when I tried to explain to them something. He looked like he meant it.

My family liked making lists. After Dad got laid off and he and Mom started their company together, they sectioned off a part of the living room and got a bunch of whiteboards and started making a lot of to-do lists. They would cover one whiteboard, and then another, and then finally they got this wallpaper that was itself a whiteboard. I'd go downstairs to watch TV and see a bunch of scribbles and arrows everywhere. Dad liked to draw arrows. Mom had this handwriting that was half-cursive and half-wasn't, so I could barely read it.

Viv liked to make a lot of lists, too. In high school, she had like four to-do lists going at any given time. She moved at the speed of light, Dad said. She worked until one in the morning, and when I woke up in the middle of the night to go get water downstairs, I could see the light to her bedroom still on through the crack in her door. She was always running. "I'm going to do this volunteering thing by the beach," she'd say on Saturday mornings, grabbing her piece of toast to go. Or, "I'm going to Philz Coffee to study with Laura." Last year, when Mom and Dad were mad at each other to the point where they didn't want to have dinner together, she would quickly slip out the door to go study, or to go work with a friend, or something. And I didn't want to have to pick whether I wanted to eat with Mom at five-thirty (which was when she liked it) or eat with Dad at seven (which was when he liked it), so I ate at six-thirty and made myself Bagel Bites.

Now, after Viv got into college and graduated from high school, all she had was one list. And it was the list of the things she wanted to do before she left home. She'd come back one evening, shaking sand out of her tote bag and sweats from going to the beach. Or she'd go out the door, wearing a black top with her cheeks covered in glitter for a concert. Or a friend would swing by in a car and she'd bundle up her backpack and a sleeping bag for a weekend camping trip.

Mom and Dad said that she earned it. That the hard part was over and it was finally time for her to have fun. Viv seemed to have everything to do this summer and none of them took place at home.

I didn't write many lists. I only kept two, and both of them were in my head. I didn't like to think about them a lot, which meant that I ended up thinking about them all the time, as I was falling asleep or during random moments in the day like helping Mom do laundry or brushing my teeth. One of the lists I made was called Reasons Why Naomi Stopped Hanging Out with Me. There were five things on that list already, like how I could have talked about my ye-ye less and tried to become friends with Emily and tried to listen to the music she liked listening to.

And there was the one list I made last summer.

It was called Things I Could Have Done to Save Ye-Ye. And it was about how I could have planned to leave his apartment in the afternoon of that day in late January instead of the morning. How I could have stayed instead of taking the Muni home when Ye-Ye told me to go home because he was dizzy and needed to lie down. How I could have called Nai-Nai and told her to run home instead of saying nothing and calling Naomi to talk about something silly and unimportant when Ye-Ye was six and a half miles away, dying of a stroke. How, maybe in that world, if I'd done all those things, Ye-Ye would still be here today, and it wouldn't be too late.

Last August, Scavenger Hunt Stop 3

I spy a thing that takes many a shape and size.
I make things hide and invisible to the eye.

There is nothing better than a Japanese stationery store.

That is, unless it's a Japanese stationery store built across the street from a hardware and gardening store, because it was definitely easier to convince Mom and Dad to let us go if Dad could also peruse an oddly large collection of garden clippers across the street.

In fact, Viv and I once declared this store as the best place to get stuck during a zombie apocalypse. There were approximately three hundred different corners to get lost in, rows of stationery and trinkets to occupy us, and a shelf of the best Asian snacks including my favorite bear cookies stuffed with chocolate to last us for at least months.

(The second best place to get stuck at during a zombie apocalypse is a Costco. For obvious reasons.)

But this was Viv's fifth year of not coming to the scavenger hunt. Which was *fine*, but it made me just a little sad that our favorite hideout became one of Ye-Ye's scavenger stops and she wasn't even here to see it.

"Look at the origami paper they have now," I said, pointing at the shelf to our right. Ye-Ye loved collecting origami paper for no reason. Sometimes he folded paper cranes with it. Sometimes he wrote little notes on it.

Ye-Ye leaned over. "You want some?"

"It's okay," I said. Ye-Ye sometimes gave me fancy origami paper as presents, and I always let it stack up in the corner of my bedroom drawer because it was too pretty to touch and I was scared of messing it up.

I refocused on the clue. *I spy a thing with my eye.* . . .

I looked up at Ye-Ye. "From where?"

"Let's . . . say the starting point is the back of the shop."

I headed toward the back of the shop, passing rows of small lined-stationery bundles and tapes that were patterned with hearts and flowers. *Nai-Nai would like these,* I thought. She always loved patterns. I passed scrunchies embroidered with cat ears and tea steepers in the shape of floating walruses.

Ye-Ye, Viv, and I used to play I spy a lot. We'd stand somewhere and Viv would think of something and we would take turns guessing. Viv always guessed my objects instantly and then would go and pick the hardest things to see because she had like 20/15 vision or something.

Now, I stood in the back of the store, making sure that I was turning, slowly, taking everything in.

Invisible to the eye.

Many shapes and sizes.

I knew what it was.

"It's the eraser shelf."

Ye-Ye's smile confirmed my guess.

The eraser collection took up a whole corner of the store.

There were so many kinds of erasers that there were drawers for each kind. The pieces of the erasers detached from each other. I held up a sushi eraser and a small xiǎolóngbāo eraser that you could detach each individual bun from. Viv used to love these. She had a collection of eraser animals that she would line up at the edge of her desk. But at some point after eighth grade she gave her entire collection to me, so I had a sixteen-course eraser meal in my drawer and a whole eraser food chain on my bookshelf.

"They had new eraser animals," Ye-Ye said. "I figured you'd like it. You can get one, if you want."

I glanced over detachable hedgehogs and lions and elephant erasers. I looked at Popsicles that you could pull the sticks out of and macarons that separated into three parts. I arranged all the food on a small eraser tray. I kept looking back at the one in the shape of the strawberry cake. The detail was perfect, down to the yellow dots as strawberry seeds and the whipped cream.

"You like this one?" Ye-Ye looked over.

I held it in my hand. It was so small in my palm. "Viv would have liked it," I said.

I looked up and met Ye-Ye's eyes. An unreadable shadow passed over his expression, and then the corners of his eyes relaxed and he nodded. "I think so, too," he said. "You want to get this one for her?"

I paused, weighing the eraser in my hand. "I don't know if she even wants this anymore."

There wasn't a particular reason why Viv stopped coming to the scavenger hunts. One year she had a robotics competition, and the next year, she just didn't feel like it. And that was that. Ye-Ye didn't seem fazed at all, or not at first. He just said that she outgrew them. Just like how she outgrew cool erasers and handed everything in her collection to me without a bat of an eye. Maybe he sounded kind of sad. I don't know. It was years ago. I wondered if I would wake up one day and not want to go on a scavenger hunt. I couldn't imagine that.

In the end, I picked the hedgehog eraser and Ye-Ye paid for it at the register. And then we went back up the stairs and Ye-Ye went to use the bathroom. I looked around for a while. And then I dashed back and picked up the strawberry cake eraser. I brought it to the cash register and dug my birthday money out of my pocket and paid for it. And I kept the strawberry eraser in my pocket with the hedgehog and as Ye-Ye came out of the bathroom, my fingers curled around it to keep it a secret.

EIGHT

I PRACTICALLY FLUTTERED up the steps to Naomi's house, my gift clutched in my hand and my phone in the pocket of my jeans.

Everything had fallen into place. Nai-Nai agreed to let me sleep over, as long as she came to pick me up tomorrow morning after she went shopping for her Friday groceries. Mom and Dad wouldn't have to know a thing.

Naomi, Mia, and I always had a yearly sleepover on Naomi's birthday. Her dad would grill the best veggie burgers in their backyard and her mom always made these homemade crispy kale chips that somehow made kale taste good. At the end of dinner they'd bring out a carrot cake for Naomi with cream cheese frosting, and we'd eat slices until we were practically sick. Naomi and Mia and I would stay up late into the night on a sugar rush and play card games or truth or dare, which, for Naomi and me, was mostly truth or truth. Mia was the only one who took dares, which involved prank texting her aunt in Chicago in the middle of the night, or drinking a bowl of Reddi-wip with a straw, which she took like a champ. Mia and Naomi talked about their crushes while I listened. Last year, Naomi told us about a crush she had on someone in the boys' soccer league. Mia told us she was crushing on Lola Nuñez, who sat behind her in math class and wore butterfly clips in her hair. We'd always end up too jittery to sleep, so we'd watch a bunch of funny videos until we finally all crashed on top of our sleeping bags. In the morning we'd stumble downstairs. Naomi's dad would make us French toast with strawberries while I'd pet Mango, their cat, and Mia would try to draw whipped cream faces on her French toast.

I wondered when the three of us would hang out again. We could never really make three-way video calls work because the timing never worked out. Either Mia or Naomi was always busy with something. And Mia hadn't mentioned visiting San Francisco in a long while.

I texted Naomi, **here.**

The wind chime next to her door clinked in the breeze. I tucked my hands inside the pocket of my hoodie.

Maybe this year was weird, but it would all become okay. Naomi still wanted me to sleep over. We could still play truth or truth. We would FaceTime Mia in and eat too much carrot cake.

Her mom answered the door. "Oh, Ruby, hi! I'm so glad you're here." She had the same green eyes and heart-shaped face as Naomi, except her brown hair was streaked with gray. She pulled me into a hug. "The others are in the living room. Dinner is ready in just a bit!"

Others?

Laughter streamed in from the living room. And that's when my heart dropped into my stomach.

Because Naomi hadn't just invited me—she'd invited half of her soccer team.

My palms started to sweat. The back of my neck felt all hot. Naomi bounded up to me and wrapped me in a hug. "Ruby!" she said, as if we hadn't spent the last two months of school practically ignoring each other. But it felt nice to hug her again, and she smelled like the coconut shampoo she always used. "You came!"

"Happy birthday," I said, weakly.

"Thanks." She took the present and added it to her pile right next to the door. Without skipping a beat, she turned to me and said, "Okay, so we're trying to figure out if a guy Jenna is into is trying to ask her out or not." She leaned toward me. "It's been going on for *months*. Oh, and this is Delaney, Jenna, Em, and Meg. Guys, it's Ruby."

Her friends barely glanced up. Two of them flashed a smile at me before huddling around their phones. I squished myself into their circle, sweating through my hoodie.

"Marco's Snapped you multiple times," Em told Jenna, a girl with short dark brown hair who seemed engrossed in her phone.

"Right, but also he always keeps leaving me on read for like days."

I was saved by a purr at my elbow. Mango nudged her dappled head against my hand. I gave her chin scratches, just like she always loved.

Okay. I was fine. Mango would keep me company. I occupied myself with petting the cat until Naomi's mom came in and told us that her dad was bringing the burgers in from the grill.

"Thank you so much, Mr. Malone," Em said, as she piled two burgers on her plate. She scooted right next to Naomi at the table. I remembered last year, when Naomi was talking about how good this girl from our class, Emily Hunter, was on her soccer team and how intimidating she was. But now they leaned in and whispered to each other. Naomi showed Em a text under the table and Em laughed. Em motioned to Jenna, who hovered around them.

Delaney laughed and rolled her eyes. "It's the guys' soccer league," she said, dabbing her fries in ketchup. "There's always some kind of drama going on over there."

I smiled, grateful. "Yeah," I said. "I can imagine."

After dinner, Naomi's dad brought over the carrot cake, and Naomi grinned as we all sang happy birthday and she blew the thirteen candles out. Her parents took pictures from different angles. This year, I could hardly take a couple bites before I felt full.

To be honest, I kind of wished I was with Nai-Nai right now. At least I'd be comfortable on the couch and watching an episode of the Chinese drama. Instead I was following Naomi and her new friends up to her bedroom.

"All right," her friend Em said. "Truth or dare?"

Most of it was just people daring each other to call up their other friends or their contacts on their phone. Em dared Naomi to eat a spoonful of hot sauce. Meg asked about Jenna's most embarrassing moment last week, and then everyone laughed at the question like it was some inside joke I wasn't part of. I was half thinking about going downstairs to see what Mango was up to when Naomi turned to me.

"So, Ruby," Naomi said. "Truth or dare?"

"Truth."

She grinned at me, and I was just reminded of how much she'd changed this past year. She was perfectly tanned from her days playing travel soccer, her brown hair streaked with highlights from the sun. She clasped her hands, and I noticed her chipped nail polish. She used to wear rings that Mia and I had given her for her birthday last year, but now they were gone. "Hmm. I'm thinking."

Jenna piped up. "Current crush?"

Naomi knew I hated being asked about crushes. I shrugged. "Don't have one," I said flatly.

She raised an eyebrow. "You sure?"

I swallowed. "Yeah."

Her friends smiled at me half-heartedly. Naomi quickly turned to Em. "Okay, your turn." And then she tilted her head and raised her eyebrows, as if some kind of secret message passed between them.

Em leaned back and giggled. "Aw, Naomi, come on."

"Truth or dare, Em."

"Fine." Em sighed. "Dare."

"Okay," Naomi grinned triumphantly. "While we're on the subject of crushes, I dare you to text the boy *you* like."

Delaney and Jenna looked over, as if they all knew what was about to happen.

Em's cheeks turned red. She stared at the ground for a moment, as if she were psyching herself up. And then she looked right up at me.

"Hey, Ruby, do you happen to have Josh Fang's number?"

I froze.

Josh.

As in, my cousin. Who was on a travel soccer team. Josh, with his confident smile and his way of making himself the star of every room.

"Um," I said. There was no way I could get myself out of the situation. "Yeah, I guess." I handed over my phone.

"Oh, my gosh, *thank you*," Em gushed, typing furiously. All her friends hovered over her. I felt physically ill. She let out a shriek and threw her phone on Naomi's bed and covered her eyes. "I texted him."

And suddenly it all became crystal clear to me. Naomi didn't want me here because she wanted to be friends with me again.

She wanted me here so her friend Em could talk to Josh.

As truth or dare went on I quietly slipped out of the room and went down into the kitchen. I opened up Naomi's fridge where the water dispenser was. It was late at night, and everything was dark. I filled my cup and sat on the floor, my back against the fridge. I felt something brush at my elbow and jumped, only to find Mango, staring at me.

"Hey," I said. Surprisingly, she flopped onto her back and let me give her scratches. I took sips of the water, still sitting there against the fridge.

As I tossed and turned in my sleeping bag that night, all I could think of was that this used to be *our* sleepover. Me and Mia and Naomi. Friends since second grade. We'd carved our names into the backyard trees and named Naomi's potted plants and eaten countless slices of carrot cake. But now Mia was on the opposite side of the country. Naomi had moved on. And I was trailing behind, my eyes smarting under the covers of my sleeping bag.

Last August, Scavenger Hunt Stop 4

In the Saturday morning square it's stop and go;
surround all sides to beat your foe.

Ye-Ye had one of those small cardboard tables made out of shipping boxes. We crossed the square to take a seat at one of those benches and Ye-Ye pulled it out of his backpack. As we sat on either side of the armrests, I helped Ye-Ye prop up the table on the armrest so that the two cardboard legs touched down on either side.

"What are we doing here?" I asked. "Eating? Playing a card game?"

"Think, Ruby."

Stop and go. Did it have something to do with traffic? Was it a game of red light, green light? What was Ye-Ye up to?

Surround all sides. I looked around me at the other old men playing chess in the square and I knew it. "Oh! Weiqi?"

Ye-Ye grinned and reached into his bag and pulled out a makeshift game board, a grid with nine deep bold dots at the intersections of certain lines.

So *that* was the clattering in his backpack. It was all the go pieces.

Ye-Ye smiled. "Care for a game with your lǎo ye-ye?"

I grabbed the set of black chips from him and sat down on the bench, one knee propped up and tucked under my chin. We set down our pieces on the bold dots. White after black after white. Click, click, click.

There used to be a time when I couldn't sit down for a full game. I'd grow restless after ten minutes. I'd try stacking the pieces or making wild patterns, even as Ye-Ye explained to me that it was about creating space and pockets for yourself—making sure you weren't surrounded on all sides, and taking over parts of the board, bit by bit. It was mostly about patience, something that Ye-Ye seemed to have all of and I none of. But then a couple summers ago I got bored and watched a bunch of YouTube videos on it, and I actually won a game somehow. I never let Ye-Ye live it down.

Ye-Ye loved this game. Sometimes Nai-Nai would play with him. She would shift around in her seat and go back and forth to get snacks. Ye-Ye was like a statue in the sunlight now, his chin resting against his fist. I nestled my cheek against my knee and hugged my leg, eyes trained on the board. Every once in a while, I peeked down at my phone, which was hidden under the table. Mia was texting me and Naomi a list of everything she was packing in her boxes.

I looked up as I heard the clatter of chess pieces being swept up. "Just surrounded your pieces," Ye-Ye said. "I've got that corner now."

I tucked my phone back under the table, keeping an eye on it. I leaned over the board for a long minute. The wind blew, scattering a newspaper across the square. I set a piece down, surrounding his one piece. It was a small victory, but I'd take it.

I heard the click of a piece and looked up to see Ye-Ye sweep even more of my pieces off the table, with a small smile. My phone buzzed. I saw Mia's text pop up in the group chat.

"Something on your mind, Ruby?" He nodded toward my end of the table.

I sheepishly shoved my phone into my pocket. "Sorry." I leaned back over the chess board. I watched him put down his piece. "Dad was telling me something the other day about a robot that could play Weiqi."

Ye-Ye raised his wispy eyebrows. "Really?"

I nodded. "And it could beat the best human player."

He smiled to himself. "Would you like to play against a robot?"

"No," I said. "I like playing with you." I saw an opening on the board, and then swept up his pieces. "And it's harder to beat a robot."

"Ai-yah!" Ye-Ye said, leaning over the board in surprise. "I was going easy on you, that's all."

"Of course." We heard the tinny blare of a radio playing old Chinese music coming from the other end of the park. A flock of pigeons flew overhead. The board filled up. My phone buzzed in my pocket.

"I'm scared of seventh grade," I found myself blurting

out, before Ye-Ye set his piece down. He took it back.

"Why?" He straightened up.

"My friend Mia is moving," I said. "Her dad is taking another professor job. In New York."

"That's far," Ye-Ye said.

"She keeps saying that she'll try to convince her dad to move back in a year," I said. "But even if she does, she's going to miss everything. She's going to miss the seventh-grade dance. And our matching Halloween costumes that I'd planned. And—" My breath hitched. "What if she never comes back?"

Ye-Ye leaned over the board and laid down a white piece. "It's never a bad time to branch out to new friends. Maybe it'll be hard at the beginning, but there will be good changes, too."

"Do people always change?" I said. "I feel like I've always stayed the same."

"Is that true?" Ye-Ye said lightly. "I feel like you're a bit taller this year."

I laughed. "Okay, besides that. I don't know." I felt like everyone around me changed a lot. Like my friends. And my sister. And my parents. I gestured to the game board in front of us. "I mean, Viv used to be excited about all this scavenger hunt stuff. Now she doesn't come."

Ye-Ye paused, his eyes carefully on the board. "She's just growing into herself," he said. "And so are your friends. And so are you. And sometimes, in the course of that, things become different than they used to be."

"But I don't want things to change," I said. "I want things to stay like they were. And I don't want Mia to move, because it's always been us three. Ever since second grade." I liked how all three of our lockers were next to each other. Or how we sat across from each other in homeroom. I leaned back.

"Well," Ye-Ye said. "At least you could call her."

I absentmindedly put down a piece. "True. We said we were going to FaceTime every evening. We calculated the time difference and everything. She's three hours ahead, so the best time to call her is at five my time and eight hers."

"See?" Ye-Ye said, setting down a piece. "My Ruby is smart. Always thinking of solutions." He leaned back. "Good game."

"What? But we didn't—" I paused as I leaned over the board. "Oh." Ye-Ye had closed in on the last corner, and there was no other move I could make.

"Next time," Ye-Ye said, "you'll beat me." Then he mimed moving his arms like a robot, and I laughed.

We cleared the pieces off the board and into the boxes, and then Ye-Ye folded up the board and the makeshift table and tucked them back into his backpack. I pulled out my phone and checked it for a text, but there was nothing.

"Seventh grade seems like a hard time." Ye-Ye patted my shoulder. "But don't worry about Mia. True friends will always come back to you eventually."

107

I nodded.

Ye-Ye said, "How's your sister, by the way?"

"Good. Why?"

He shrugged. "I just wanted to ask. I don't see her much."

"Oh," I said. "Me neither. And we live in the same house."

"Busy, is she?"

I exhale, long and slow. "Yeah. Her and everyone else, it seems like. Except you."

He laughed. "I'm a retired old man," he said. "I have all the time in the world." He glanced across the street. "Want some milk tea? I'll give you your next clue there."

I nodded and followed him across the square, surreptitiously checking for texts. Still nothing. My shoulders relaxed, but my fingers still clutched my phone.

NINE

I WOKE UP before anyone else did. The curtains were pulled over the windows, but I could see the foggy early-morning light stream in. I could make out Em's messy bun peeking out from the top of her sleeping bag at my feet. I stared up at the ceiling for what seemed like hours.

I wished I could just bolt out of the house and never come back.

I checked my phone. It was 6:21 a.m.

I flopped back down. Nai-Nai wasn't coming to pick me up until nine.

Somehow I fell back asleep and by the time I woke up again, all the sleeping bags around me were empty and the smell of French toast wafted up. In the past years, that would have made me race to the kitchen. But I curled to my side. I could hear Naomi and her friends. I didn't want to go downstairs and have to talk with them again.

I heard a purr somewhere above me. Mango blinked at me with yellow eyes.

I slipped back under the flap of the sleeping bag. Here, everything was warm and safe. Like a cocoon.

Mango brushed past my head.

"Okay, okay," I sighed, emerging from the sleeping bag. "I'll get up."

I put my hoodie on and rolled up my sleeping bag, carefully putting it in the corner like I always had. I walked downstairs, Mango padding at my feet.

"Good morning, Ruby!" Naomi's dad grinned. "I saved some French toast just for you. I added a couple new things this year."

Naomi and her friends sat around the table, talking.

"We could go up to Stinson Beach for a day," Delaney was saying. "My family always does a barbecue there."

"Ooh, or down to Santa Cruz," Em said. "And hang out on the boardwalk!"

Naomi's mom glanced at me. "Hey, Ruby," she said, keeping her voice light. "What are you up to these days? Any fun summer plans?"

I shrugged mid-bite. This French toast somehow was even *better* than last year's. "I'm seeing my grandma a lot."

"You should come to the beach with us," Delaney piped up.

"Yeah," Naomi said, like an afterthought. "It'll be fun."

"I'm . . . busy," I said. "Gotta . . . help my sister with some college stuff."

Naomi's eyebrows knit together. "But Viv doesn't go to college until August."

"We have so much time before then," Delaney said. "Next weekend?"

Em didn't say anything. She just ate her French toast.

"I'm busy then. I have to help my mom . . . with a thing."

Wow. I was *really* bad at coming up with excuses.

"That's cool," Delaney said, giving me a small smile. I decided that I liked her. Maybe, in another universe, we could have been friends and she wouldn't have ditched me like Naomi did. And suddenly I wanted to be somewhere, anywhere, except this house. I checked my phone. 8:43. I pushed myself up. "Sorry, I gotta go."

"Aw, really?" Naomi's dad glanced over. "You want more French toast? You usually eat ten of these things."

"My grandma's supposed to pick me up," I said. "She's coming soon. Thank you for having me." I went to the corner and picked up my backpack. I could feel the stares of all of Naomi's friends.

I pushed past the door and had almost left when I heard, "Ruby, wait."

I turned and Naomi stood there, awkwardly. "Just wanted to say thanks for coming." She paused, not quite looking me in the eye. "And, uh, text me if you can make it next weekend, okay?"

I stopped in my tracks. "Seriously?"

She raised her eyebrows. "What?"

I should just go, I thought. But I blurted out, "You don't want me there. Or here, for that matter. So why don't you just say that to me instead of pretending to want to invite me to places?"

She glanced quickly behind her, and then at me. The conversation in the kitchen had gone silent. Naomi let the door fall shut behind her. She frowned. "Ruby, I—"

I stepped closer to her. "You only wanted me here so Em could text Josh. You knew that I had Josh's number."

Her eyes widened, as if she realized how much that had hurt me. But then her expression shut down and she crossed her arms. "I don't get how that's such a big deal. We all were just having fun."

I straightened up. "I don't want to come to Santa Cruz with you," I said. "Or anywhere. Because I don't think I matter to you anymore." I took a deep breath. "And we both know it."

"Okay," Naomi said. "Is this about me being friends with Em?"

"What?"

"I invited you so you could get to know my soccer friends, Ruby. I know you don't really like Em, for whatever reason. But I thought you could get to know her and you guys could, I dunno, get along." She set her shoulders. "Besides, just because we don't hang out that much

112

anymore doesn't mean we can't still be friends."

Really, if I could spew fire out of my mouth right now, I would. All over her wind chimes.

"Do you really not see it? We haven't talked in *months*, Naomi. You don't really want to be friends with me. You just wanted something from me. And that's not the same thing."

And before I could see the look on her face, I turned around and marched away from her porch.

All this time and I'd been hoping that somehow, there would be a big miraculous talk or something that would fix Naomi's and my friendship. I thought that it was just a matter of time, and Naomi and I would be friends again.

I scanned around me and checked my phone. It was 9:10 and there was no sign of Nai-Nai. There was the park down the street where Mia, Naomi, and I used to go all the time. I walked over there, climbed the small rock-climbing wall that led up the platform for the slides, and sat there.

Ye-Ye said last year on our scavenger hunt that sometimes, people drift away. But I always thought that they drifted back, that time would pass, and the tides would push us to each other again. Now I felt as if I were far out at sea, on an island all by myself.

I glanced at my phone. 9:44. Nai-Nai was never this late to things. And she wasn't answering my calls.

I picked up the phone and dialed her number once again. It rang through to voice mail.

I stood up, my heart racing.

Maybe Nai-Nai was on her way. But something felt off about this, and I had to get home.

The Muni stop was only a couple blocks away. Going home was just a straight shot on the N line, and then two more stops on the bus. I had taken this dozens of times with Ye-Ye, but never alone.

I scrounged up the five dollars I found in my backpack to buy a ticket. The streets were busy, full of people on their way to their Friday morning work. I sat on the train, clutching my backpack to myself.

What if Nai-Nai was already on her way?

What if she just forgot? What if she just went to the senior center like she always did?

But she wouldn't. Nai-Nai only went to the senior center from Mondays through Thursdays. Fridays she did her shopping and watched TV at home.

There was no reason why Nai-Nai shouldn't be answering her phone. I'd given her the address. Even if she never used her cell phone, she still had the landline that had a ringtone you couldn't miss.

I fought to keep the panic from rising in my chest.

I'm on my way home, I'd texted Nai-Nai. *Headed back on Muni.*

I got off and switched to the bus. Maybe I should call May. Or text her. But I didn't have her number. The bus bumped all the way up Montgomery Street, and when I got off, I ran straight to Nai-Nai's apartment complex. Hands shaking, I fit the key and turned the lock. I walked into an empty apartment.

Nai-Nai wasn't there.

I frantically scanned the living room. Her cell phone lay on the table. But Nai-Nai's purse wasn't there, which meant that she was out.

But out *where*?

I locked the apartment behind me and ran back down the stairs.

I checked the markets on Stockton first. She said that she would pick me up after she did her Friday grocery shopping. I went through the fresh produce section, past the boxes of cabbages and yams and leeks. I stopped by a box of ripe lychees—Nai-Nai loved those. But she wasn't there.

I walked down the block, weaving around the crowd. Every time I saw permed gray hair, I stopped in my tracks. But it wasn't Nai-Nai.

Think, Ruby. I paused, taking in a deep breath. *What would Ye-Ye do?*

He'd go find May to help.

I could do that. I turned and walked down the street, and then turned onto the block where May's Bakery was. May spent her Fridays at the bakery, since Fridays and the weekends were busy.

I should never have gone to Naomi's sleepover. It was

all for nothing. And now Nai-Nai was somewhere in the middle of Chinatown.

Just when I was about to head into May's, I saw a flash of floral pants.

I stopped on the street. "Nai-Nai!"

The floral pants stayed in place. I sprinted down the street, my backpack thumping against my back.

And I practically crashed into my nai-nai.

She grabbed me by the arms, her expression alarmed. "Ruby-ah! Where were you? I was looking for you everywhere! I was scared you had run off!"

I stopped. "I was at Naomi's house. At her sleepover. I thought you were coming to pick me up."

"Sleepover?"

"I was going over to Naomi's house for her birthday. Remember? You dropped me off yesterday."

Nai-Nai's eyebrows were still knit together in confusion.

"Remember? Naomi? My middle school friend?"

And suddenly Nai-Nai met my eyes. "Oh. Your school friend! Sleepover. Yes. That's how . . ." she trailed off, looking around here. "Right. I was going to the bus stop. I knew I was going there but I forgot what for."

"But . . ." I looked around me. "This is the way to May's Bakery and the senior center. The bus stop is on the other side of Chinatown."

"That's not true." Nai-Nai looked around slowly.

"I just came from the bus stop," I said. "You were going the wrong way."

Was this a prank? Was Nai-Nai playing a joke on me?

But Nai-Nai wasn't laughing. She kept looking up at the buildings, and then back down again. She looked plainly at me. "I was, wasn't I? Tiān-nah."

I shook my head. "Let's go home, Nai-Nai."

I retraced my steps and we walked back to Nai-Nai's apartment. We shuffled up the stairs, slowly. Nai-Nai looked at me. "How was your friend's house?"

"It was . . ." I stopped. An awful feeling sank into me. I had left Nai-Nai. I'd gone off to my friend's house and left her all alone in the city. "Fine. It was good to see her."

We made it to apartment 3B. I unlocked the door and we walked in.

"Wah, I left my phone at home." Nai-Nai chuckled. "Thank goodness you found me. Your nai-nai's brain is getting fuzzy."

I smiled to reassure her but I couldn't help the worry that knotted in my chest.

How could Nai-Nai forget a bus stop in a city she'd lived in for over forty years?

Nai-Nai and I did end up going shopping for her groceries. I helped her put them away and we spent the rest of the day mostly watching even more episodes of the Chinese drama. She shuffled around the kitchen, patting down the countertops with a towel.

She seemed like she was before. She put the spices in the right cabinets. She put the tofu on the second shelf of the fridge, where it belonged. When I saw her reaching up to retrieve a container of soup on the top shelf, I rushed in and helped set the container on the counter.

"Ai-yah, Ruby," Nai-Nai said. She looked up. "Your nai-nai is fine. Don't look so worried like that."

I nodded and sat back at the kitchen table, fidgeting with my fingers. I couldn't not be worried. I had missed all the warning signs for Ye-Ye that day: his dizziness, his off-balance walking, the way his cheeks sagged. Now I knew I needed to keep track of things that didn't seem right.

After lunch, Nai-Nai went into her room for a nap. I sat on my bed, my stomach twisting into knots, my thoughts chasing each other in circles.

I shouldn't have gone to Naomi's house. I should have stayed here. I should have gone shopping with Nai-Nai. I should have come home early. I should—

I rested my cheek on my knees and hugged my legs as close to me as I could.

And the other question stayed in the back of my mind. *What if this happened again?*

I needed to tell Dad about Nai-Nai getting lost. And Mom. When would I mention it? I would bring it up at dinner, maybe, tonight when Dad picked me up and drove me home. But then I tried to imagine how the conversation would go. They would ask me what had happened. I would have to tell them about Naomi's sleepover. They would get mad, I realized. My heart sank. Of course they would. They'd get angry at me and at Nai-Nai for letting me go.

I didn't know what would happen next. Would they yell at Nai-Nai? It wasn't her fault. But would they stop letting me stay at Nai-Nai's place? Would that leave Nai-Nai by herself again? I couldn't leave her alone. If she was left alone maybe she'd forget more things and no one would be around to help her remember.

Maybe I wouldn't tell them, for now. I would tell them eventually. For now, I'd just keep watching Nai-Nai.

I stayed at the kitchen table until I looked across to the living room and stared at Ye-Ye's desk. And an idea crept into my mind.

There *was* something I could do. I crossed over and sat down on Ye-Ye's swivel chair. I clutched the cracked leather armrests and leaned back into the cushions. I closed my eyes, and I could almost smell the green tea he used to make and the Tiger Balm that he always carried around.

Ye-Ye kept paper in the second drawer. Pens and colored pencils he kept in the top. Atlases in the bottom.

I laid out two sheets of paper in front of me. On one piece of paper, I started a list. I printed out the date and wrote down: *Nai-Nai got lost and couldn't find the bus stop.*

I looked at the other sheet of paper. Ye-Ye's map, with his pencil markings and his scribbles, was tucked back home in my bedside drawer, but Ye-Ye had a spare map of the city in the bottom drawer of this desk.

I pulled it out. I placed the piece of white printer paper over the map. And slowly, I started to sketch it out.

The thing about maps is that they look scary at first. The roads seem all jumbled together like tangled yarn. The street names blend into each other. The first time Ye-Ye gave me a map of San Francisco with his list of clues, I stared at it for what felt like an hour because I didn't even know where to start.

But slowly, you figure it out. I thought of the map of San Francisco that Ye-Ye had drawn on over the years, the colored pencil marks crisscrossing each other, the notes scribbled in the corner, and stars marking places that I would eventually know like the back of my hand. The maps became three-dimensional, changing from a messy jumble of lines into threads of favorite streets that led to where we wanted to go. Or home.

This time, I tried to re-create the map that Ye-Ye and I had made together all those years ago for his scavenger hunts. Except instead of marking down the best candy shop, or the place to watch the sunset, or the place to race toy cars, I put down the senior center and the corner shops and the Chinese pharmacy that Nai-Nai passed by every day on her way back from the grocery store. I carefully printed the location names, triple-checking to make sure that I had spelled the street names right. I drew everything down on this new map, hoping with all my might that it would, without fail, lead her home.

TEN

"HOW'D THE CONVERSATION with the landlord go?"

Auntie Lin turned toward May Wong. Nai-Nai listened intently. I looked up from where I was scrolling Instagram. I'd seen Naomi's post over the weekend but I couldn't help looking at the pictures again. There were pictures of Naomi blowing out the candles, her hugging Em, and her at brunch, surrounded by her friends. I wasn't in any of them. I'd assumed this was going to happen. It didn't make me feel any better when it did.

But I told myself there were more important things to worry about now. As in, the bakery. This was the last-resort conversation they were having, May Wong said. So if they couldn't agree on things . . .

May Wong shook her head. "We've been trying. But

they're not negotiating the rent down. And they're not budging on that."

My heart dropped into my stomach.

"The developers have been offering a really good deal. They said they're trying to turn it into an art exhibition space."

No, I thought frantically. It wasn't supposed to be like this. May was supposed to figure out a way. She always did. She—

Just then, the front door swung open, and Liam and his grandmother walked in.

"Good morning, aunties," Liam chirped. "Long time no see. Sorry I wasn't here these last couple days."

How could someone be *this* happy on a Monday morning?

"Morning, Liam," May Wong said.

"Morning, Ruby," Liam said. Thud. He started to unzip his laptop case. I shrank in.

"Hey," I mumbled.

He glanced over at me. "What's up?"

What could I say? *My best friend and I hate each other, Nai-Nai got lost for no reason, and May Wong's business is really, actually going under.* Instead I shrugged. "Nothing."

He loaded his computer up and it whirred loudly to life. He glanced sidewise at me.

"You wanna play some Rocket League? I saw you

watching last time." He reached into his bag. "I brought two controllers again, just in case you wanted to."

I shook my head.

"Are you sure? Come on, give it a shot. It's fun."

I looked up at his hopeful smile. He was just trying to be nice. I knew. I swore I knew. But before I could stop myself, I heard myself saying, "I just *don't*, okay?"

The grandmas from the other table looked over.

"I just—" I barreled through. "Just stop, okay? I don't want to play right now. Stop trying to get me to or whatever. Can't you just get that I. Don't. Want. To?"

"Ruby!" Nai-Nai said.

I stood up, the chair legs scraping the floor. I couldn't bear to look at Nai-Nai. Out of the corner of my eye, I saw the hurt written all over Liam's expression, but I couldn't look up at him, either. Liam's grandmother had a confused, bewildered look, turning to me from her grandson, and that was what made me feel the worst.

I stood. "Sorry," I mumbled. "I'm going to go on a walk."

"Ruby—" Nai-Nai said.

"Just ten minutes," I mumbled.

I could hear Auntie Lin saying, "Let her go. She's caused enough ruckus in this place already."

It stung, but Auntie Lin was right, I realized. No one wanted me here. They were all just too nice to say it. I pushed open the doors and stood in the middle of the side-walk, blinking tears back.

I paced down the sidewalk. My insides felt all knotted up. What was *wrong with me*? I tried not to think about the smile dropping from Liam's face and his wide eyes.

Of all the people to snap at, it shouldn't have been Liam. *Why* was he getting on my nerves? Was it just that he was so happy all the time? Why did he always come in like he'd won the lottery? A small part of me understood why everyone, even Auntie Lin, softened up to him. He was always nice. And I wasn't. I thought about what Nai-Nai had said, that Liam and his family were trying to adjust to the city and make new friends. It must have been hard for him. I wondered what I would have done if I were a new kid and I moved to a completely new place in the middle of March. I probably would have curled up into a ball and not spoken to anyone. I wouldn't have tried to make any friends. I probably wouldn't even have gone to school.

Which made me feel all the worse about what I had said to him.

Two seconds later, I was on my way down the block. I stopped myself at the end of the sidewalk. I turned a sharp right, and before I knew it, I was heading toward May's Bakery.

I paused in front of the doorway, shifting my weight from

foot to foot. And before I could chicken out, I walked in.

Nothing had changed. The peony brush painting was still there. The fan still roared in the corner, maybe louder than before. Or maybe it was loud now that the bakery was quiet. And on my right, the shelves were stuffed with rows of the softest sponge cake, sweet toasted coconut bread, and creamy egg tarts.

"Ruby!"

I turned. May Wong's daughter Annie was behind the counter today. Her hair was in a short pixie cut and dyed a dark purple. She looked tired but when she smiled, it lit up her round cheeks. "It's been forever since I've seen you in here!"

"Hi, Annie ā-yí." I met her eyes. I didn't know if I should tell her I knew. Instead I smiled. "It's good to see you, too."

"What would you like today?"

I pushed a five-dollar bill over the counter. "I just want an egg tart, please. Keep the change."

"Why don't I make that two?" I opened my mouth to protest, because an egg tart was two seventy-five. Annie waved it off, slipping two egg tarts into the paper bag and handing it over to me. The bag felt warm in my hand. "Second one is on the house. It's good to see you back, Ruby. Come back soon?"

"I will," I said. I had eighty-six dollars saved up from birthdays and allowance, and I was going to spend every bit of it at May's if that could even begin to help.

I could almost *feel* Ye-Ye here. "You see, Ruby," he had said once. "This city has changed, all around." He pointed out the building across the street. "There used to be a wood carving shop." He pointed down the street. "And that one there used to be a roast duck shop." He looked around. "They're all gone now. But this one place has stayed."

"Because of you," May had quipped from the counter. "You coming in every other day for coconut bread has kept this business afloat."

Now I thought about Ye-Ye again and I walked out before my eyes could start smarting. I clutched the paper bag tightly in my hand. I took two deep breaths, and then I pushed in the door of the senior center.

I walked over to the table. Liam was on his computer, off to the side. The grandmas quieted when I came over. I saw May Wong's gaze land on the paper bag. Liam looked up when I approached.

I sighed. "I'm sorry. I didn't mean to say all that."

Liam didn't say anything.

I held out the paper bag. "Truce?"

He tilted his head to his side, his expression still cautious. "What's that?"

"Egg tarts. From May's Bakery."

His eyes slowly lit up. "An egg tart truce? Okay, we're talking." He shrugged off his headset and reached for an egg tart. He took a bite and his eyes grew wide. "Mmm. Officially forgiven. These are the best things ever."

How was he so quick to smooth things over? I plopped down in the chair next to him, looking down so he couldn't see how relieved I was. "Sorry. I didn't mean to yell at you."

"I heard," Liam said softly, so that just I could hear. "About May's Bakery. I was just talking to her about it. That really sucks."

"Yeah." I puffed my cheeks and exhaled. "It does."

We sat there for a minute in silence.

"Anyway," I said. I looked at the screen. "How does this game work, anyway?"

Liam polished off his egg tart. "You *sure* you want to learn?"

I nodded. "Yeah," I said. "It seems kind of fun."

"*Sweet*," he said. "Here's your controller. You press *A* to accelerate. *X* to aim. And then you kind of just zoom around and avoid being hit. Oh, and also, you know, score goals. Got it?"

"Got it," I said. "Get ready. I'm about to whoop your butt at this."

"Hey, uh, try to score a goal before you talk smack?" But Liam was grinning.

Before he hit start, I glanced over at the table where Nai-Nai was sitting. Her eyes twinkled. May Wong smiled at me.

I wish I could tell her that before I came back, when I was standing on the corner of the street where the bakery was, I had made a promise to myself. And that promise was that I was going to do everything I could to try to help May save her bakery.

I finished my reread of *The Phantom Tollbooth* and didn't look for another book to replace it. Instead I talked to Liam. Sometimes I joined him in Rocket League. We discovered quickly that I was pretty bad at the whole scoring-goals-and-getting-points thing, but Liam was nice about it. I managed to score several goals on myself and yet he didn't ban me from playing.

Little by little, I learned more and more about him. I overheard one of the discussions between Auntie Lin and Nai-Nai one day that the reason why Liam's grandmother had come over to the States was because Liam lost his mom to cancer when he was nine, and his grandmother wanted to come take care of him. Hearing that made me feel even worse for how I'd lashed out at him. Liam had lost someone who was really, really important, too, even if he didn't talk much about it. Now I made a point to be extra nice to him and his grandmother. His version of my nai-nai.

I played games with him every morning and watched him score point after point. Around noon, Liam would put his computer away. We listened in on the conversations between Nai-Nai and Auntie Lin and May Wong and Liam's grandmother, until we basically started sitting at their table. Things accumulated on this table: Liam's laptop bag, his grandmother's yarn, May's tea thermos, my mini backpack, and two decks of cards. Auntie Lin got the most competitive over card games, even though May Wong was pretty even with her. Nai-Nai had no such luck.

"Just wait one day," she said, once May had won yet another round. "I can beat anyone in a good game of mah-jongg."

Nai-Nai was good at mah-jongg? I didn't know that.

"Tiān-nah, you still play?" Liam's grandmother said. "I sat in on my mother's games, but I swear I've forgotten how to play."

"Give me a game of poker and I'll take you all," Auntie Lin said, and everyone groaned.

"You like those games with odds and bets, don't you?" May Wong quipped. She looked over at us. "You know Auntie Lin used to trade stocks?"

"Bets make things more exciting," Auntie Lin said. She nodded over at us. "Hear that, kids? If none of us shows up next Monday, we've all gone to Las Vegas."

May Wong shook her head and Liam laughed. "I don't doubt it."

Sometime in the afternoon, after we all ate the lunches we brought, I stood up. "I'm going on my walk," I said.

Liam perked up. "Going to the bakery?"

I nodded.

"Can I come? I brought some spending money today."

"Liam," his nai-nai said. "Ruby knows the city, but you don't."

"It's only a few blocks away," I said.

"Yeah, and I'm going with Ruby."

"Let them go," Auntie Lin said. "They need to stretch their legs every once in a while."

Liam stood up. Auntie Lin still had her sharp words and hard stares, but I was starting to warm up to her a bit.

I kept a little bit of my allowance money in my phone case. I knew I needed a better plan for helping save May Wong's bakery other than chipping away at my total of now seventy-five dollars, which was probably a tiny fraction of the rent that needed to be paid, but I hadn't thought of one yet, and at least I felt like I was doing *something*.

"What are you getting today?" Liam looked around the street, his eyes wide.

I shrugged. "Probably some of their coconut bread."

"Ooh, coconut bread."

"Is that a good *ooh, coconut bread* or a bad one?"

"Do people not like coconut?"

I looked at him. "Some really don't. It's sorta like how some people really don't like pineapple on pizza."

"There are people who don't like pineapple on pizza?"

I shrugged. "My sister Viv hates it. She says fruit and pizza don't mix."

"Well, I'm sure your sister is cool and all, but her pizza preferences do make me sad."

I smiled at the ground.

"Hi, Ruby," Annie called out from behind the counter

in English. She looked over at Liam. "You even brought a friend today! I haven't seen you around."

"This is Liam," I said. "He moved here a couple months ago."

"Hi, Liam. I'm Annie."

"Hi, Annie ā-yí," Liam said. "Wow, you look exactly like May."

"Turns out we're related," Annie said. She grinned, and she had May Wong's warm eyes. "Apple didn't fall far from the tree, huh? It just has purple hair and five tattoos. Don't tell her about the fifth—she doesn't know about it quite yet." She straightened up. "What can I get you, Ruby?"

"A coconut bread, please," I said. I handed over my money, and Annie scooped the freshest, softest coconut bread off the rack. I could almost *hear* the pillowy bread give in where her tongs clamped it. A few toasted coconut flakes fell. She handed it over, and I breathed in the sweet scent. "Thank you, Annie ā-yí."

Liam got a piece of coconut bread as well. "Doh-jeh saai," he said, in Cantonese. *Thank you.*

"Mmmmm," Liam said, hugging the paper packet to his chest as we walked back down the block. "This can't possibly be better than the egg tarts, but I'm excited."

"It just might be better," I said. "This was Ye-Ye's all-time favorite thing to get from May's."

He glanced over. "Auntie May Wong told me you and your ye-ye had been coming to her bakery your entire life. Is that really true?"

"Yeah," I said. "May said that she used to have a small step stool behind the counter so I could stand on it and look at the shelves."

"Wow, you and the coconut bread really go way back."

"Ye-Ye and the coconut bread, too," I said. "He'd been going to this bakery since he was a kid, back when May's parents ran it. He used to have these scavenger hunts around the city and they always started at May's."

"Really?" Liam stopped. "Your ye-ye set up *scavenger hunts* for you?"

I nodded. "Every year, the weekend before school started."

"Every year?" Liam's eyes grew wide. "Where'd you guys go?"

I shrugged. "Places he thought I would like. He loved maps. He had a big map collection of all these cities around the world and like ten maps of San Francisco. And he lived here all his life, so he never ran out of places to go. Sometimes he'd give clues to museums. Sometimes it was the beach." I pointed across the street at the square where the old men did tai chi and played chess every Saturday morning. "Sometimes it was just places like that, to play a game of Weiqi or something. He'd been doing this ever since

Viv and I were like really little. But he'd always pick me up early in the morning and we'd go to May's first. But I haven't been back much since . . . yeah."

Liam was quiet for a while. "Your ye-ye sounds really cool," he said. "I see why you talk about him all the time."

"I miss him a lot," I said. I met Liam's eyes, and his expression told me that he understood what it was like to miss someone just that much and that painfully. "He could have shown you around. He would have bought you every single thing from May's. That's the first place he always took someone. Legend was that May's was the place he met Nai-Nai."

Liam lit up with a smile. "Really?"

I nodded.

The dimple deepened. "That is quite possibly the cutest thing I've ever heard."

I shrugged. "It really was his favorite place."

"No kidding." Liam took a bite of the coconut bread and practically melted into the ground. "Mmm. Yep. I see it now."

"Yeah," I said.

We rounded the corner and approached the senior center doors.

"Does May Wong really have to sell that place?"

I clenched my jaw. "I don't know."

Liam was quiet. "That's really sad."

I looked up at him. "I'm going to help save the bakery."

"What?"

"The bakery," I said, my voice steadying. "It can't go. I'm going to figure out a way to help May Wong save it." There. I said it. Now there was no going back.

ELEVEN

"I HAVE A new game idea," Liam said when he came in the next day.

I glanced up from my set of cards. Auntie Lin had brought her Uno deck, and I had just gotten two plus-four cards stacked on top of each other.

"Hold on, Liam," Auntie Lin said. "We're playing this game through."

"Oh, that's just because you're down to your last two," Nai-Nai said.

Liam loaded up his computer. "Have you ever played something called GeoGuessr?"

I said, "Geo-what?"

"Oh, you'll love this." His computer groaned to life as usual. Liam's fingers flew over his keyboard. When he turned it around to face me, there was a picture of a random road surrounded by trees. I forfeited my now-twelve-and-counting cards and peered at the screen.

"Where's this?"

His eyes lit up with a mischievous look. "See, that's the point of the game. They drop you in a random place in the world somewhere and you have to figure out where you are. Or, well, as close as you can get."

I leaned closer. "Where do you even start?"

"Well, for starters, I try to look for road signs. Sometimes I can figure out the language or narrow it down to a continent or something. If I can't see any signs, then I try to look for cars." Liam clicked somewhere on the screen, and we zoomed in farther down the road. "If it's driving on the left side of the road or something, then we know it's not the US. Mostly you just move up and down a lot before you make an educated guess. It's about putting the little clues together."

"Do you ever guess right?"

"Oh, I've never gotten it exactly right. That's like looking for a needle in a haystack. My best guess has been within probably ten miles of the actual place."

"Okay, well, we're going to find it." I glanced at the screen. "I'm guessing Italy."

Liam gasped. "Really? How'd you figure it out so quick?"

I shrugged. "Just a gut feeling."

"Okay, we are *not* relying on your gut."

"Fine." I peered closer at the screen. "I see a car."

"Car!" Liam said. We scrolled closer.

"It's on the right side. Rules out the UK."

"And Australia and New Zealand and all that. Okay, okay, we're getting somewhere."

Liam zoomed farther down the road. "Car, car, more cars . . ."

"Road sign!" I pointed at the map.

We both stared at the blue road sign for a moment.

"That's a Cyrillic language," Liam mused. "Based on the characters. I'm guessing a country in Eastern Europe. Or Russia."

"I didn't know you were an expert in Cyrillic languages."

"I'm really not," Liam said. "I just play this game way too much for my own good. Like, sometimes I watch YouTube videos of people playing this."

I laughed.

"What?"

"Nothing."

"I see you judging me," Liam said. "But if I recall correctly, *someone* said they were going to guess the right place."

"Okay, fine. I'll be helpful. Here, scroll down. I think I see a building."

Twenty minutes, three more road signs, and a whole long discussion about Eastern European roundabouts later, we finally settled on eastern Bulgaria as our best guess. By this point, Auntie Lin was peering over our shoulders.

"Ready?"

"Born ready."

Liam dropped the pin and put in his guess. "And . . . no way. It really is Bulgaria."

"Crushed it," I said. "Oh. We're five hundred kilometers off."

"But we got the right country, so that's basically a jackpot. Next round?"

Auntie Lin scooted her chair closer. "What's this?"

"It's GeoGuessr," Liam said. "Wanna play?"

Auntie Lin brightened at the mention of another game.

"Here." Liam moved his computer to the larger table. "So this game drops you anywhere in the world, and you have to figure out exactly where you are. You kind of have to poke around. You can use road signs, license plates, anything to try to narrow it down."

Auntie Lin cracked her knuckles. Even Liam's grandmother looked over from her knitting project and smiled.

"Maa-Maa knows it's my favorite game," Liam said, grinning. The screen refreshed, and we were in the middle of a winding road, with mountains stretching tall on either side.

May Wong leaned in. "Now, where on earth is this?"

"Himalayas," Nai-Nai said. "Alaska. Colorado. Chile."

Liam looked up. "Are you just listing places with mountains?"

Nai-Nai looked sheepish. "Maybe."

"There's a car." Auntie Lin's eyes were intently trained on the screen. "Oh, wait! Another one."

It took us forever to come to a guess. Half of us thought it was somewhere in the Andes, whereas Auntie Lin insisted it was Nepal. Nai-Nai was just like me. She threw a guess out there and hoped for the best, whereas Auntie Lin scrolled in so intently on every single detail of the surrounding geography, you would have thought she was looking for treasure. But at some point I glanced up and realized that for the first time, we were all huddled around our table, watching Liam as he clicked through the map.

Ye-Ye would have loved this, I thought.

And when we landed three hundred kilometers from the actual location—in Nepal—Auntie Lin's eyes practically beamed with joy.

"Again?" she said.

Liam refreshed the page.

"So, how does one work this instant gram, anyway?"

Auntie Lin was tapping on her phone with her pointer finger. I was staring at my notebook, trying to think of ways to help May Wong's bakery. So far I'd written nothing. Liam wasn't here that morning, not yet, anyway.

It was weird, how the senior center seemed so loud when I first arrived. Now it was kind of quiet.

"May would know," Nai-Nai said. "Her bakery runs one of those social media accounts."

"It's all Annie," May Wong laughed, pushing up her glasses. "I don't even know the login."

"Ruby might know," Nai-Nai said.

Auntie Lin looked over at me with an unreadable expression. She arched her eyebrow. "You know?"

I nodded. "Instagram? Yeah. People use it all the time to post about their lives." I only made one so that Mia and Naomi could tag me in pictures and send me funny videos, but now neither happened and I just spent time on there scrolling mindlessly. I'd commented on Mia's post of her at her summer ballet showcase and she replied with a heart emoji. I must have looked at Naomi's birthday post at least ten times. I don't know why I did that to myself.

Auntie Lin waved me over. I begrudgingly settled into the chair next to her. "Okay. Well, first, you make an account."

I guided her through the steps and she tapped on the screen. "Now you edit your profile picture," I said. "Do you have any pictures of yourself?"

Auntie Lin hesitated.

"We can take one," I said. "Here." I gently tried to take the phone from her. She gripped it for a second more and then she let go.

I took an unsmiling picture of her and set it as the profile. "Perfect," I said. "Well, it's time for your first post."

She snatched the phone back. "Post? Who said anything about posting?"

"What are you making an account for, then?"

She handed her phone to me. "To follow my daughter. She gave me her username the other day. Esther Zheng. All lowercase."

I looked up. "You have a kid?"

"Two of them. Why do you look so surprised?"

"I . . . yeah. Okay." I guess I'd thought that Auntie Lin had always existed as the lady who lived alone around the block, and all she had raised were two cats. I typed in her daughter's username and turned the phone around. "Is this her?"

Her expression softened. "Oh, yes. This is. How can I follow her?"

"Already done." I pointed at the screen. "See?"

She scrolled through. The woman in the pictures had Auntie Lin's sharp nose and bright eyes. In one picture she smiled, holding up a plate to the camera. In another, she had her arms crossed over a white jacket.

"Is she . . . a chef?"

"She owns a string of restaurants in Chicago," Auntie Lin said. "She wrote a cookbook, too. Her reviews are all over magazines. She showed me." She tapped on one of the first pictures, where her daughter was leaning over a plate of noodles. There were pictures of dishes that made me hungry, pictures of her bundled up and pointing at a Christmas tree, and video clips of her. "She was on the *Today* Show. Five thousand people liked this." She shook her head in awe, her tongue clicking. "Wah, she's famous. No wonder why she told me to get on this website."

Nai-Nai looked over. "She looks just like you."

For once, she smiled. "That's what they always told her. I loved hearing it and she hated it. Always wanted to be her own person."

"What about your other kid?"

"Oh, my son? He works in banks like I used to. I'll probably get to see him around Christmas, if he's lucky." She shook her head and let out a brittle laugh. "That's the thing about kids. They grow up and go to college and then fly away from you for good."

I thought of Viv and deflated, just a little.

"My daughter, though, she's coming for my birthday next week. She'll probably come around here."

"Well," May Wong said. "I would love to meet her."

Auntie Lin scrolled on her phone for the good part of the next hour until the bingo game, her frown lines smoothing. When I went to get water, I brought her a cup, too. She didn't look up. But after bingo, when she got a Hi-Chew candy as a prize, she didn't tuck it inside her purse like she used to. She gave it to me. "Keep it," she said. "I have enough, anyway."

I took the Hi-Chew, and inside, I was glowing.

TWELVE

"HOW ARE YOU going to help May save her bakery?"

Liam and I sat at the park where Ye-Ye had taken me to play chess, our paper bags of char siu bao, egg tarts, and fried dough fritters in our laps. Music blared over the radio. A group of old men played a game of cards, intently hunched over a makeshift table.

I took a big bite of my char siu bao, savoring the tangy barbecued pork. I chewed for a moment. "I don't know. I was trying to think of ideas."

"And?"

"I have no clue. I might try to talk to my parents about it. I haven't come up with much." All my internet searches just told me how big of a problem this was, with Chinatown businesses being bought up left and right. Talking about it reminded me that I really had no idea what to do.

And according to May, the bakery would be turned over at the end of summer.

"Well, I was talking to this librarian the other day," Liam said. He finished his egg tart and polished off the crumbs. "She's an amateur historian. She says this has been happening for a long time."

I nodded at the ground.

"She says there's ways to reduce the rent. You can, like, apply for something called a Legacy Business Registry. If you apply and get accepted, they can stabilize your rent so you don't have to pay more. Or they can help you out with money."

I glanced up. "Really?"

"They have a whole website and everything. I don't know if it can save the bakery, but I think it could do something." Liam sat up. "I want to help with this."

Behind us, an uproar burst from the table as one of the old men tossed his cards down. I craned my neck and turned back around. "You sure?"

He nodded. "Yeah. I see how much the bakery means to you. I don't know how much I can do to help you with your plan, but I can poke around the library. I'm also great at googling stuff, if I might say so myself."

"Well, the thing is, there really isn't a plan right now."

"Then we'll make one."

I couldn't resist a small smile. "Okay. Let's do that."

"Project partners," Liam said. "Take two."

145

I laughed. "I wouldn't count the first time."

"I think we made good progress on the civilization of Mesopotamia."

"Well, you had to be extra good at reading and ditch me."

"They moved my homeroom," Liam said. "I would have never ditched you. It would have been a stellar project. You were actually one of the nicer project buddies."

Really? I carefully looked at him. If he considered *me* to be nice, then . . . "You said you had a nosebleed that day in the nurse's office. Were you . . . okay?"

"Oh, that," Liam said, shaking his head. "I actually get nosebleeds all the time. It's, like, an allergy thing. I don't know. But, yeah, gym knockout didn't really go my way. I ruined my Teenage Mutant Ninja Turtles shirt. It was sad."

I gave him a look. "That's what you were sad about?"

"What! It's my favorite shirt!"

"Okay, okay, then I'm sorry about that, too."

"Thank you. My shirt really appreciates it."

I polished off my char siu bao. Liam asked, "What happened to *you* that day?"

The bun got stuck in my throat. I swallowed. I picked the crumbs off my lap, each and every one. "I, uh. Got caught for ditching school."

"Really?" Liam's eyebrows shot up. "You? Of all people?"

I turned toward him. "What do you mean, *me* of all people?"

"I dunno. I didn't think you were the ditching school type. You know, the one they make all those movies about. Like *Ferris Bueller's Day Off*."

"Okay, not like *that*. I was caught for ditching to have lunch outside school."

"Oh."

"Yeah. I just . . ." I raised my shoulders, then let them drop. "Didn't want to eat by myself in the lunchroom. That's all." It sounded so embarrassing, now that I said it. "And I liked going to the nearby park. And then it just became a whole big thing."

"Oh." Liam didn't bat an eye. "I mean, that makes sense. The lunchroom is kinda scary."

"Where did you sit?" Come to think of it, I never saw him there.

"I spent my lunches in Sully's classroom."

"You ate with the math teacher?"

"Not exactly. You know how people make up tests during lunchtime in Sully's classroom? Well, I just took a book there and ate my lunch. It was kind of nice. No one really bothers you."

"And you did this every day?"

"Not always. Sometimes I'd sit in the social studies classroom and eat lunch. Take it from someone who's moved a lot. Sometimes teachers will be extra nice and let you eat lunch in their classrooms, as long as you don't bother them. I mean, I totally would have sat with you, but I guess I always thought you were with your other friends or something."

"Yeah, well." Pigeons fluttered above us, and we jumped in our seats. I stared at my shoelaces. "I don't really have those other friends anymore."

"What happened?"

"My friend Mia moved to New York because her dad switched jobs," I said. "And my other friend Naomi started hanging out with her soccer friends more. I don't know. Maybe it's because of me. I probably could have been funnier or listened to better music or been better at talking to people or better at soccer or something. I don't know. Maybe she then would have still wanted to be my friend." Now I was just rattling things off that list I'd made of reasons why I thought Naomi stopped hanging out with me.

"Uh, Ruby? You know that you don't have to be good at things to get to be someone's friend, right? They should just want to be friends with you. For, you know, you."

I looked up from my shoelaces.

"I mean, I think you're one of the coolest people I know." Liam grinned, his dimple deepening. "Even if you score on yourself in Rocket League all the time."

"Not *all* the time!"

"You did it just this morning. It was kind of sad."

"My controller slipped!" I opened my mouth and closed it. "And I'm not bad at all games. I'm better at Mario Kart."

"Oh, don't even challenge me on Mario Kart. You don't know who you're up against."

"I just did."

"Well, prepare to get lapped," he said. Just then, Liam peered at his phone. "Maa-Maa is asking where we are," he said. "We should probably go back. We should also probably tell May Wong we wanna help."

"Yeah," I said. "Thanks for . . . joining in."

"Anything for the coconut bread." We stood. As we swept away our crumbs, Liam said, "Just so you know, you're officially invited to sit with me. Anytime. If you want."

"Yeah," I said. My heart felt lighter. "I will."

Before I stood up, I checked my phone as well. A notification popped up, saying that Naomi had posted a new picture. I clicked on Naomi's profile and then caught myself before I could see what she'd posted. I clicked out and put my phone away—and went to join Liam.

May Wong smiled at us while we told her that we were thinking of ways to help her keep the bakery afloat. Liam told her all about what he had found out from the librarian. After we were done, May Wong reached out and took both our hands in each of her hands. She gave my fingers a squeeze. "Thank you for thinking about this," she said. "It means a lot to me. It really does." She sighed. "But it's more than rent. There's a lot of debt riding on the bakery, too."

Her eyes looked wistful. They weren't lighting up like I thought they would.

"But—"

"Annie and I are trying to think of the future of the bakery," May Wong said. "What's ahead of us. Unless something drastic happens, I don't think anything could change by the end of summer. But it's very kind of you two to look into this. Really."

Liam and I exchanged a glance. I raised my eyebrows. *What now?* Liam's shoulders shifted in the tiniest shrug. *I don't know.*

"Is it just me, or does May seem kind of eh about the idea?" I asked Liam later, while we were away from the tables and huddled next to the water dispenser.

"I don't know," Liam said. "Maybe she just wants to sell it?"

"She *doesn't,*" I said. I pressed the lever and water trickled out. "I know that. Nai-Nai said that she's faced these kinds of problems in the past. But she always finds a way. I just don't know why she doesn't want us to help."

"Well, she didn't exactly say that she doesn't want our help," Liam said. "She just said it would take something drastic for her to keep the bakery."

I turned to Liam. "Oh. You're right."

Something drastic. What could that be? I thought about it all afternoon, even after Nai-Nai and I had gone home for the day. The Legacy Business Registry could help with the rent. But May said she didn't just need help with the rent. She had a lot of debt, too.

I lay on my stomach on my bed, charging my phone with its one hour of battery life. I wondered if people around Chinatown knew that the bakery was struggling. I was sure they all would want to help out.

I sat straight up. We needed a fundraiser. Just like the one Naomi and Mia and I had done last year for the conservation fund. Except this time, it would be for the bakery.

I texted Liam:

what about a fundraiser for may's

in addition to the legacy business

we could send out emails and knock on doors and post all that stuff

I didn't even have to wait two seconds before Liam replied, **Oooh. That's a really good idea!**

I hopped up on my feet, my heart getting lighter. Liam and I were going to do it. We were going to prove May wrong and show her that she could save the bakery, after all. I practically leapt out of my room and into the kitchen to join Nai-Nai, who was making dinner. She shuffled around the kitchen, transferring the vegetables from one dish to another, humming. She had on a patchwork sweater that she had sewn herself and bright red pants. It was a relief to see the color seep back into her daily wardrobe. "Oh, you're back! How would you like to play some music while we cook?"

Nai-Nai hadn't played music in forever. "Sure." I pulled up my phone. "What music would you like?"

"No, *music*," Nai-Nai said. She pointed to the CD rack. "You pick."

I slid an unmarked CD out of its case and pushed it into the player. After a few moments, the notes of the piano and a Chinese ballad streamed out.

Nai-Nai waltzed through the kitchen, swathed in the bright colors of her sweater, cupping my face as she sang. And in an instant she was the carefree Nai-Nai I knew. The sun in the room. She laughed as she peeled the cucumbers, and even though I didn't know many of the words, I danced along.

After this CD wrapped up, Nai-Nai told me to put in another one. The orchestra swelled up to the sounds of ABBA. This I recognized. We spun in circles while the dishes sat on the counter, getting cold.

"Turn the knob up, Jeanie!"

I stopped spinning. "What?"

"Turn up the music," Nai-Nai said. She stopped. "What?"

Jeanie was my aunt's name. My dad's sister. Who lived in Texas.

"Ruby," I said. "Nai-Nai, I'm Ruby."

She frowned at me for a moment, confused. "Ruby?"

"Your granddaughter," I said. I felt my chest tightening. I searched her face for any hint of recognition, any sign that it was all just a fluke. "I'm not your daughter, Nai-Nai. I'm Ruby. Your granddaughter."

Did Nai-Nai forget about me?

"Ruby," Nai-Nai said slowly, and a light of recognition dawned in her eyes.

"Yes," I said. "I'm Ruby."

"Of course you are," Nai-Nai said.

"You called me Aunt Jeanie's name."

"What?" Nai-Nai shook her head. "I would *never* do that."

She marched over and turned the music up. But I wasn't in a mood to dance anymore. Later that night, in the glow of the bedroom lamp, I pulled out the list of things I'd been observing about Nai-Nai.

And I wrote, in shaky pencil, *Nai-Nai forgot my name.*

Last August, Scavenger Hunt Stop 5

Among the sea of colorful threads,
find the one that fits your Nai-Nai best.

"Colorful threads," I said to Ye-Ye. "It has to be some kind of clothing thing, right?"

He peered at the paper and then smiled at me and shrugged.

"It has to be." But what did a *sea* of it mean? Was Ye-Ye talking about a clothing store? "Or sewing?" Nai-Nai loved to sew. She made my Halloween costume every year. She made Viv a flowery stitched sweater for her birthday, and sometimes I snuck into her room to try it on because it was so soft. I stared at the clue, and then I glanced up.

"*Oh*. It's the fabric store she loves." She'd taken me there before. I squeezed my eyes shut, trying to remember it. I thought of the bright red sign out front and the big letters that hung down three stories. My eyes flew open. "Britex! That's the name."

"Good thinking, Ruby," Ye-Ye said, grinning. "That was an easy one. But that's only the first part."

We walked up the streets. It was the middle of August, but sometimes in the mornings, the wind rolled in and it would get cold all of a sudden. I took my jacket out of my small backpack and put it on. I sort of remembered the path to the place. There was a narrow street that took us there, where the buildings rose up and were so close together that sometimes I wondered what it would be like if there were a zip line between all the roofs.

The bright red store sign was as large as I remembered it and impossible to miss. I opened the door, and suddenly it was a different world.

"Wow," I said.

I'd been here several times and it never got old. Colorful fabrics stacked to the ceiling, all around us, in bolts and swaths and patches, from deep purple to light yellow to sheer pearly blue. I reached my hand out, and my fingers brushed thick wool and thin mesh cloth that was decorated with almost-lifelike stitched butterflies.

"You used to spend hours in here with Nai-Nai," Ye-Ye said. He pointed to the corner. "Remember the velvet wall?"

I walked over and observed the small boxes of velvet stacked on top of each other. A box of sequined velvet seemed to shimmer in the light.

"Okay, now we just have to find Nai-Nai something," I said.

"Exactly. I was trying to pick up some surprise gifts for our anniversary and I thought you could give some expert opinions," Ye-Ye said.

I glanced around. *What would Nai-Nai want?*

Was it the deep green satin?

Or was it the dark red velvet?

Or was it the light blue fabric with clouds sewn on it?

I wandered down the aisles, imagining the cloths for different things. A prom dress for Viv. A sweater for Mom with the soft chenille. A bag from the cloth with the funky mushroom prints. I glanced at Ye-Ye. "Is this really her favorite place?"

Ye-Ye nodded. "One of them. This is one of the first places she found in San Francisco, and she kept coming back ever since."

I thought of Nai-Nai, always sitting in a pile of her craft projects, bouncing from hobby to hobby every month. It made sense why she loved this place so much. "I always keep forgetting that Nai-Nai didn't grow up here."

"She likes to say that she stayed by accident," Ye-Ye said. "And then she liked it so much she just never left."

"Because of you?"

"Well, kind of." Ye-Ye put his hands in his pockets. "Did I ever tell you about how Nai-Nai and I met?"

I shook my head. "Not really."

"We met in New York, actually," Ye-Ye said. "I thought I wanted to be in New York and study architecture because I wanted to design those big fancy buildings. So I went to college there, even though the rest of my family wanted me to stay in California. Part of me loved New York, but I was very cold and lonely out there. The first time it snowed, I thought it was the most wonderful thing in the world. The snow felt like feathers. And then it got cold and slushy. The snow finds its way into your shoes and you just want to do anything to get warm. So I would always go down to the coffee shop below me." He smiled. "And your nai-nai worked at the coffee shop on the weekends. The coffee was terrible, but it was hot and warmed me up, and so I always went down to that shop." He straightened up. "Well, I have to admit. Sometimes I didn't really *need* the coffee. Your nai-nai was just easy to talk to."

"And then what?" I asked. We turned away from the bolts of fabric and wandered toward the ribbon aisle.

"Well, at some point she asked me why I came into the coffee shop so much. And I told her it was to get warm, and she said, 'Well, you don't have to get warm by drinking bad coffee.' So she invited me to this place in their Chinatown that her family liked a lot. And after drinking the oolong tea from that shop, I never went back to get coffee again."

"Ye-Ye," I said slyly. "I think she asked you out."

"I suppose she did," Ye-Ye said, the tips of his ears turning pink. He straightened out the red ribbon. "She showed me her Chinatown, and I told her about mine. She took me to her favorite Chinese bakery and I told her about May's. She took me to eat lā-mièn—at this tiny noodle shop that her family friend owned, and it had the most delicious beef noodles I'd ever had. I told her about the wood carving store and the shop that had the best roast duck. She told me about moving from Hangzhou to here when she was ten. She made fun of me for speaking Mandarin with such a bad

American accent and I told her that my ba spoke Cantonese and my ma grew up speaking Mandarin, and so I wasn't very good at either."

I stopped. "And then?"

He shrugged. "And then we . . . lost touch for a while."

"Really? But the story was getting good!"

"I had to come back to help take care of my mother," Ye-Ye said. "And your nai-nai stayed in New York."

"Did you call her?"

"We couldn't call very far distances back then," Ye-Ye said. "And I didn't know where to write her."

"So that was it?"

"Well. You lose a phone number, or someone moves places, and it's a miracle that you find each other again."

"But you did," I said impatiently.

"Yes, we did."

"How?"

"It was your nai-nai, actually. She was visiting a friend in California. In San Francisco. They walked into China-town for lunch and then Nai-Nai saw the brush painting store. And then they walked a few blocks and saw the place with the roast duck, and then they found May's Bakery."

"No way."

Ye-Ye nodded. "Your nai-nai told May Wong about me, and May rang me up on the phone and told me that an old friend was here to see me. And then I got to the bakery and there she was."

"She found you!"

"She did," Ye-Ye said. "She's a resourceful one, your nai-nai. She told me she just found places along the way that she remembered me telling her about. She called them her little hints."

"And then?"

"Well, now it was my turn to show her around," Ye-Ye said. "And Nai-Nai liked it so much that she came six months later and never left."

"Awwww."

"It all worked out in the end," Ye-Ye said, smiling. He glanced around. "Anything catch your eye, Ruby?"

I was peering at a shelf up top, where violet fabrics were bundled together.

And then there it was.

There was a light purple satin up in the corner that rippled in the light, with flowers stitched in. I pointed up. "I want that one," I said.

Ye-Ye looked up. "Wah, Ruby," he said. "She would love that one."

We retrieved it off of the high shelf and bought it. I looked at the shelves one last time, taking in the bright patterns and colors. And then, with the bundle tucked under Ye-Ye's arm, we pushed open the doors and headed out of the store.

"Did you like her?" I blurted out, as we turned and walked down the street to the bench where we'd unwrap the next clue. "That first time."

"I very much did," Ye-Ye said. "I was just too scared to tell her. And when I went back to California and lost her phone number, well—I thought I missed my chance." He smiled. "But lucky for me, she somehow found her way back to me."

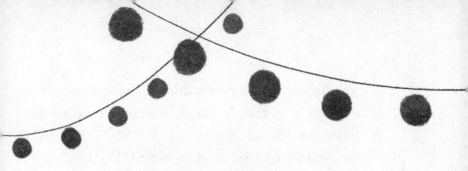

THIRTEEN

"CAN GRIEF MAKE you forget things?"

I stood in the doorway of Viv's bedroom. Sometimes, when I was little and bored, I'd go over to Viv's room, open the door, and kind of just stand there. I wouldn't really do or say anything. And then I'd turn around and go back to my room.

Viv looked up. Things were stacked up high in her room, from clothes to papers to random appliances. "No. I don't think so. Why?"

I stepped gingerly over her piles to sit at her desk table.

"Wait, no, I was going to put my laundry on that," Viv said. "You can sit on my bed."

I occupied a very small part of the corner of her bed. "I don't know. Nai-Nai seems to be really forgetful lately."

"Isn't that, like, an old people thing?" Viv said, transferring one stack to another. It was like watching a precarious game of Jenga with a lot of old tennis T-shirts. "They tend to forget some things." She knelt in front of her papers and started sifting through them.

"But she's forgetting names, Viv. She forgot mine."

Viv looked up curiously. "Is Nai-Nai . . . different? Mood swings, anything?"

I shook my head. "She's just . . . I mean, sometimes she doesn't talk as much as she used to. But I guess that one's actually probably because she's sad."

"You should tell Mom and Dad, then," Viv said, and then sat back on her heels. "They could get her a checkup."

"Yeah." I sank down on the bed. If I told Mom and Dad, they would start asking questions. And if they started asking questions, then I would have to tell them about Nai-Nai getting lost, all because I chose to go to my friend's birthday sleepover and she was on her way to pick me up.

Maybe I could just skip that part. I wouldn't be lying. I would still be telling the truth. Some of it, anyway.

I looked around. "You're taking all this stuff to college?"

"Oh, *no*," Viv said. "I'm still at the part where I'm trying to decide what exactly to bring to college. Which somehow . . . involves sorting through my high school papers." She threw her hands up. "I guess I'll just recycle it all."

I peered around the room. "And what's . . . all that?"

She rattled the list off in one breath. "Clothes I'm

bringing, stuff that's too small, dorm decorations, clothes I'm bringing part two, and clothes that I'm trying to figure out if I want to bring or not. A big maybe-pile." Viv pulled her hair back into a short ponytail and went back to sorting through her clothes, humming to herself. I stayed curled up on the bed. I wasn't sure if I should stay or go.

Viv looked up. "How's Nai-Nai otherwise? How's the senior center?"

"Actually? Not bad. They're all nice to me now."

"Oh, yeah?" Viv focused in on a checklist. "What do you even do there?"

"Mostly card games. Sometimes they just talk. May Wong goes there. You know May. And then there's this other grandmother, who comes with her grandson, and he's in my grade and everything. And there's also Auntie Lin, who is kind of grumpy but she's been nicer to me lately. She gives me her bingo candy."

"Aw," Viv said. "That's cute."

I rested my chin on my knees. "We should get ice cream sometime."

"Sure," Viv said.

"When are you free?"

Just then, her phone rang.

"Oh, shoot. Laura is FaceTiming me. Where is it?" Viv scrambled through her clothing piles and then fished out her phone. She tapped on the screen and shooed me away. "Hey."

I slid off the bed and picked my way through the clothes

piles, back to my room. I lay in bed for a while, listening to Mom and Dad talk downstairs. I thought about telling them about Nai-Nai. Maybe this was the right time. But then I thought again about all the things that would happen and my heart sank. They'd make me stop seeing Nai-Nai. They'd think that Nai-Nai couldn't take care of me. But the truth was that I needed to be with Nai-Nai. We took care of each other.

I wouldn't tell them, not now. I brushed my teeth and started thinking about other ways to help out with May's Bakery, and wondered if I could ask Viv about it. Right before I went to bed I walked to Viv's door to get her advice. But she was still on the phone.

"You *have* to come visit me next year," Viv was saying. "I don't know how I'm going to survive college without you. I'm going to miss you so much."

Her friend Laura said something, and Viv laughed. I turned around and padded back to bed.

Back when Viv and I were younger and she was just old enough to babysit me, we used to do this thing that she called traveling. She would take chairs in each room of the house and line them up, like airplane seats. We would sit in those chairs and rock back and forth, like a plane was taking off. She would cup her hands around her mouth and pretend to make the pilot announcement. I would close my eyes and imagine accelerating on a runway. We would lean back against the chairs and I could almost feel the bottom of my stomach drop a little bit, like how it felt when Mom and Dad drove down one of those big, hilly streets.

And then we opened our eyes and we were wherever Viv said we were. We put on paper hats and called them berets and we were in Paris, where we pretended to look out the window and imagined the Transamerica Pyramid to be the Eiffel Tower. Viv would then take me down the stairs on the next leg of our trip around the world. We would open our eyes to a packet of moon cakes and lychees and we were back in Nai-Nai's hometown of Hangzhou, where we'd only been once. And then for the last leg of the trip, we would cross over to the living room, where we'd pretend to buckle into the sofa and open our eyes to what Viv called Antarctica. She lined up our stuffed penguins and laid out ice cream. I ate so much ice cream that I got brain freeze. Viv rubbed my cheeks to try to get rid of it.

That summer we went everywhere. We pretended to go to New York and ate microwaved frozen pizzas. We pretended to go to the beach. We lay down on our towels in the patch of sun on the floor, and Viv told me that someday, when she could drive, she'd take me on a road trip.

"Where?"

"Anywhere," she said, her palms over her eyes. "My social studies teacher takes a road trip with her family every summer. They just hitch a big RV to their car and they go anywhere they want. I'll let you pick some of the places."

I opened my eyes and looked at the map on the wall. I didn't know many places. I only knew state names, because I had to memorize them in a song.

Viv's eyes snapped open and she looked at the red rubber watch on her wrist, and then at me. "We gotta catch our flight," she said. "Come on. We're going to London."

And then she was scrambling up and bounding across the room. I looked away from the map. I pushed myself to my feet and hurried after her, and that was kind of how things had been ever since. Viv running and me trying to catch up.

FOURTEEN

AUNTIE LIN WAS especially quiet that Tuesday. I didn't notice during the morning because Liam and I were huddled in the corner, peering at his computer screen. May had said that something big and drastic had to happen to save the bakery. So we had half a Word doc of ideas in front of us, trying to brainstorm other ways in addition to the grant and the fundraiser to raise money. Once we could come up with a solid plan, we'd present it to May. She would realize that of course the bakery could be saved, and she wouldn't have to sell it to the developers.

By lunchtime, Liam and I had run out of steam and we went to join the grandmothers. I knew something was wrong when Auntie Lin didn't say anything during bingo, and even though she still gave me the candy she won, she didn't smile. She didn't play cards. And when Liam asked how she was doing, she said shortly, "Fine. Why does everyone keep asking?"

May Wong looked up. "Your daughter is flying in sometime this afternoon, isn't she? Does she need us to pick her up?"

Auntie Lin didn't say anything for a moment. "She moved her trip back. She's coming next month."

"Next month?"

"The opening of her restaurant got delayed," Auntie Lin said. "She wanted to see it through." She set her lips in a line. "I'll call her this weekend. She's busy and working. She'll be here next month, probably. Or I'll fly to go see her."

"Well, we can't wait to meet her, whenever she comes," Nai-Nai said diplomatically. I didn't say anything. I watched Auntie Lin read from a book she'd brought. I caught the tight set of her lips and the deep lines between her eyes.

The thing was, I could sense what she was feeling, even if she was quiet about it. I remembered sitting on Viv's bed yesterday, practically invisible among her mountains of clothes. I almost *see* Viv's mind already three thousand miles away, thinking about moving in and making friends. I knew what it felt like to be left behind. My heart suddenly felt like it was wringing itself out. Because the thing was, Nai-Nai had my family. And Mrs. Wong had her bakery and her family. Liam had his nai-nai and his dad. But Auntie Lin had no one. I thought about her sitting alone on holidays with her two cats and with the TV cranked all the way up, wondering when her kids would fly back to see her.

An idea came to me.

One way or another, Auntie Lin was going to celebrate her birthday.

"Are you sure that May's Bakery qualifies to be a legacy business?"

"I think so," Liam said. "I talked to the librarian about it again some more the other day." He ticked off the points on his fingers. "It's been operating for more than thirty years, it contributes to the neighborhood history, and it's an important part of the community." He looked at me. "Right?"

I nodded. "Everyone has heard of or been to May's." And I couldn't imagine the community without it. None of us could.

"Okay. I have some forms with a lot of questions. I can email you them or something. There's just a couple steps."

We were sitting on the benches at the park, except it was quieter today. There weren't any card games going on behind me. Even the pigeons had decided to flock else-where. "What do we have to do?"

"Well, for starters, we need to get a nomination from someone from the Board of Supervisors of the city."

I deflated a little.

"Don't worry," Liam said. "I'll take care of that. I'm good at emailing adults stuff."

"Really?"

"Oh, yeah. I've emailed, like, landlords before. You just have to make sure you use fancy words and spell things right. And you always sign off your email with *regards* and your name." He looked back at the form. "Okay, this next thing you have to help me out with. We need to tell the story about the bakery and how it's contributed to the community."

"That we can do," I said. "I can talk about my scavenger hunts with my ye-ye. And I can ask my dad to see if other people remember things. He can help email people." Maybe. Probably. If he wasn't too busy working. He must have had good memories at May's, too. Right? "And May has a bunch, I'm sure. She loves telling stories." There were the ones she told over and over again. Like how they had to pull the step stool out for me the first times I went because I was so small. Or the time Viv and I had a coconut-bread-eating contest.

"We'll do that, then." Liam grinned. "It'll be cool, hearing the history of the bakery."

"Yeah." I smiled, tucking my hands into my pockets. It was all coming together. I'd looked up how to start those online fundraisers that people could pitch in for and design some flyers on a free website. The Legacy Business Registry, along with this fundraiser, would come up with the money May needed. "When do you think we should tell May about all this?"

"This Thursday? We could get the forms all filled out with as much info as we can before then. And get the flyers ready. And we can spend all of next week asking May about the stories."

"Sounds good to me."

We sat for a while in comfortable silence. Then Liam turned to me. "You said you always went to May's before your scavenger hunts?"

I nodded. "Yeah."

"Every year?"

"Yeah."

"What were the scavenger hunts like? Were they the same each year?"

What could I say about them? I thought about it. "They changed every year. It was always like six to eight stops. Sometimes Ye-Ye would take us to the coast. He did a scavenger hunt like that one year. Viv—my sister—was really into marine animals at the time, so the first stop after the bakery was the tide pools. And it ended at Lands End."

"What's Lands End?"

"It's the place that overlooks the sea," I said. "It has all these rocks that make up this circular maze, right by the water," I said. "'The end is where we begin to meet / everything is a circle by the sea.' That was the clue."

"Ooh. Cryptic."

"Yeah. Ye-Ye liked to be all clever about the clues. That was the last year Viv did the scavenger hunt. She got bored of it. But then the next year Ye-Ye had the scavenger hunt in an art museum, so he left clues in and around the museum. Another year it was the Exploratorium. So, like, the clues would lead to a planetarium or the butterfly exhibit. Other years would have a free library, or a mural somewhere. No two years were the same."

"How did he find all the places?"

I shrugged. "He just *knew*. I mean, he'd been here his whole life. I guess he just kind of knew this city inside and out."

"*Wow*," Liam said, his voice incredulous. "I wish I came along on those scavenger hunts."

"You would have liked them," I said.

"Tide pools sound cool. Maybe I should ask my dad if we can go sometime."

"I can give you a list of all the places we've ever gone, if you want," I said.

"Ooh, I'd love that. I've been trying to get my dad to take us around here," Liam said. "I think he's still making up his mind about if he wants to stay. I'm trying to convince him to."

Stay?

I looked up at him. "What do you mean, stay?"

Liam shrugged. "I dunno. I don't know if my dad will want to move in three months or a year or something.

Maybe he'll want to stay. Maybe he won't."

"You really move that much?"

Liam glanced at me. "Yeah. I don't mind it, really. As long as Maa-Maa's comfortable with the place."

"Why?"

"He switches jobs a lot," Liam said, sighing. "And he doesn't stay in a place for more than two years, tops. After my mom passed away, Dad sold the house. He said it was because of money, but I think it's also because our home didn't really feel like home to him anymore. So we moved into an apartment on the other side of Tacoma. And things were fine for a while, I guess, but Dad always seemed like he was itching to move somewhere. A different city. So we packed up and moved near Portland. Maa-Maa moved from Guangzhou to come help take care of me. I started middle school and I thought, well, maybe this place is it. But then Maa-Maa didn't like the Portland suburb we were in. She doesn't know a lot of English. She really couldn't go anywhere and someone said a lot of mean things to her at the grocery store. So finally we moved here. I guess it all makes sense. And I'm glad Maa-Maa is more comfortable here. She can speak Cantonese with everyone. But nowhere has felt like home since the one with Mom and Dad. We move, and I think this place is it. But then he packs everything up again, and we move again." He sighed. "It's all cool, though. I've gotten to see lots of places. And my Cantonese is getting better."

His voice sounded light, but there was a hard edge behind it. I stared at the lone pigeon that landed on the bench across from us. I thought about all the things I wanted to say to him. Finally, I said softly, "I'm really sorry about your mom."

"Thanks, Ruby. That means a lot."

I exhaled. "My nai-nai said that once after Ye-Ye died. About the house thing. She went to her friend's place in this beach town near Los Angeles for months. She said she couldn't bear to take walks without him. That—" My breath hitched. "That it's hard to be home without the person you love."

"Yeah. It was too quiet for my dad, I think," Liam said. "He missed her singing."

I looked at him. "What'd she like to sing?"

"Random songs that were on the radio. Sometimes she'd forget lyrics, so she'd make them up. She'd grab a water bottle and pretend it was a mic."

"Really?"

"Yeah." Liam laughed to himself. "Yeah. She would. She—" He stopped himself.

"What?"

"Never mind."

"Wait. Tell me more."

"You sure?"

"Yeah."

"Well, she was really good at card games. She loved

newspaper crosswords. She made really good pies, but we didn't really know her recipe. Sometimes my dad and I try to re-create her pie. It never tastes as good as it used to. We think it's something with the butter. I think we got the filling right, but the crust is always a mystery." He sighed, puffing his cheeks out. "And sometimes I try telling myself what she was like. The other day I was trying to figure out what kind of snack bars she really liked, and I couldn't think of it for hours." He paused. "And I really, really wish she was here." He glanced at me, his feet fidgeting, his hands balled up in his pockets, like I did when I was trying not to cry. "Sorry, I guess the last part was more about me."

"No, it's okay. Thanks for telling me all that."

He met my eyes. "Thanks for letting me talk about it. A lot of times people don't like it when you bring it up. They get uncomfortable and try to talk about something else."

This is why Liam didn't talk about it much. Because he was worried about how it would make others feel. That kind of broke my heart, because I knew what he meant. It had happened so many times—with teachers, with family members, with Naomi at lunch—when I brought up Ye-Ye. So I said, "Your mom seemed like a really cool person. I wish she was here too."

"She would have loved you. And she would have made you sing Beach Boys in the car with her."

I laughed. "I totally would have. Only for her."

* * *

On the way back, I asked, "Does missing people make you forget things?"

Liam glanced up. "What do you mean?"

"I don't know. You said you forget things sometimes. But my nai-nai's been forgetting a lot of stuff lately. Names, or where things are around the house. I don't know if that's . . . because of Ye-Ye. If losing someone does that to your brain or makes you confused."

"Hmm," Liam said. "I never forget names or where things are around the house, though. Does that happen to your nai-nai a lot?"

I shook my head. "Not really. Maybe. I don't know yet."

"Come to think of it, I did remember her calling Auntie Lin by the wrong name the other day. She just kinda gave her a weird look."

"Yeah, I . . ." I started to tell him about the sleepover and Nai-Nai getting lost, but the guilt rose up and I shook my head. "Never mind. My sister says that this happens to you when you get older. Maybe it's, like, an old-person thing."

"Maybe," he said, but he looked at me carefully, like he was worried.

We headed back down the street. The walk back felt different than the walk here, somehow. Maybe it was because after Liam and I had talked, things had changed. We now worked on stuff together and told each other all kinds of things about our families. I would never ignore him in a hallway again or tease him in my mind.

"Hey, Liam?" I said, once we were close to the senior center.

"Yeah?"

"This is kind of out of the blue. But want to throw a birthday party with me?"

He turned and his eyes grew wide. "It's your birthday soon?"

"No," I said. "A surprise birthday party for Auntie Lin. I just feel like she needs one."

"Oh," Liam said. And then, without skipping a beat, he added, "That sounds *awesome*. I'm in."

FIFTEEN

"CAN YOU STILL come over tonight? I've bought all the ingredients to make the chicken, but I don't know the first thing to do with them."

"If you *really* need help with that recipe," Auntie Lin said, rolling her eyes. "Of course I'll help."

"*Thank* you," Nai-Nai said emphatically. She adjusted her bright leaf-print dress and gave me a sly look.

The plan was set in place for that Wednesday night. Auntie Lin was going to come over to Nai-Nai's apartment later, thinking that she needed to help her make a steamed chicken dish. We'd given Liam a key to the place and a pack of blow-up balloons. "Go wild," I said. "Deck the place out."

"On it."

Liam and his nai-nai and May Wong all pretended to

leave early to go home. And then it was just Nai-Nai and Auntie Lin and me.

"The important thing," Auntie Lin was saying when we were climbing the stairs, "is to steam the chicken for just long enough that it's cooked, but still tender." We turned around to Nai-Nai's door. "And then—"

She stopped in Nai-Nai's doorway.

The house was awash in light from the setting sun. Balloons settled on the counters and piled up on the couches, and the streamers swayed from the fan breeze.

May Wong and Liam and his nai-nai stepped out from the kitchen.

"Surprise!" Liam burst out.

Auntie Lin clapped a hand to her mouth. She turned around to face us, her mouth open.

Then she looked to the table. Plates filled every inch, brimming with pot stickers and steamed buns and vinegar-soaked cucumbers, with platters of braised pork and scallion pancakes. There were bowls of mung-bean soup and plates stacked high with coconut bread and sugar donuts and sesame balls and egg tarts.

Auntie Lin looked at us. "So the dish—there's no—"

"Of course not," Nai-Nai said. "We wouldn't make you cook for your birthday, would we?"

Auntie Lin's face stayed a picture of shock, but her eyes softened.

"Surprise," I echoed softly. "Happy birthday, Auntie Lin."

* * *

Here was the thing when you had dinner with a Chinese grandmother: they would never, ever let you leave a meal unless *they* were positive you were full. Which meant that with four Chinese grandmothers I was stuffed with stir-fried noodles and beef soup and yóutiáo positively to the point of bursting, and they were still not done piling food onto everyone's plates.

"Here," Nai-Nai said, giving me another helping of noodles. "Are you still hungry?"

"Bǎo-le," I protested. "I'm so full already."

Auntie Lin's tongue clicked. "Too little food," she said, and then gave me another helping of noodles. "Look at Liam."

Liam was busy inhaling the noodles. He peered up from his plate, his cheeks stuffed.

"And you have to save room for the cake," May Wong reminded us. After the plates were cleared away, she went into the refrigerator and got the cake.

Auntie Lin peered over. "Is that a mango cake? And are those . . . flower-shaped mango slices?"

May Wong laughed. "Well, you do like those mango candies."

"What, are some hidden in there?"

"Not quite. I'd like you to keep some of your teeth."

Auntie Lin's eyes shone as we lit the candles, and as we sang her happy birthday, in English, she looked around at us in wonder. For once, she was smiling. Beaming.

"Now in Chinese," Liam said. "And make a wish. Another one." We laughed and sang the birthday song again, in Mandarin, and then Liam and his nai-nai and May sang it in Cantonese. "Another wish!"

She leaned over and blew out the candle. The cake was light and airy and the mango mousse melted on our tongues. Before I knew it, I was reaching for another slice.

It was funny, how I had once thought that the only way I would have fun was if Naomi and I hung out. And how I thought that hanging out with four grandmothers was the worst thing that could happen to me all summer. Because while I was counting the minutes at Naomi's birthday sleepover, the hours at Auntie Lin's birthday party flashed by. Suddenly it was nighttime and we were all full, and my stomach was hurting from laughing.

Liam and his nai-nai were the first ones to leave, because they lived across the city and his nai-nai's bedtime was early. I walked them down to where his dad's car was waiting to pick them up. Liam's dad waved to me, with the same dimpled smile. I waved back. I turned back to Liam. "Thanks for helping out. And for helping put up all those decorations."

"Are you kidding me? This was fun. We should have dinner parties all the time."

"Yeah," I said. "We should." I glanced up. "How'd you get through all those balloons?"

"I might have gotten a little dizzy," Liam said. "But birthdays are birthdays. I can't *not* go all out."

I went upstairs to the sound of laughter. Nai-Nai turned the lights on. Auntie Lin went to the corner and her eyes lit up. "You have a mah-jongg set here?"

Long story short, we all stayed up for another two hours. Auntie Lin quickly ran through the rules for me, which didn't really end up mattering anyway because Nai-Nai and I started making up rules that drove Auntie Lin nuts, May started stacking the mah-jongg tiles, and, finally, Auntie Lin gave up on taking the game seriously overall. Nai-Nai put on some music to dance, and soon the dance party turned into an impromptu karaoke showdown. May Wong belted out a heartrending cover of "Shanghai Tan." Auntie Lin and Nai-Nai sang an effortless and loud duet of "The Moon Represents My Heart," and Nai-Nai made me join in. I couldn't read Mandarin much, so I just gave background vocals. I watched Nai-Nai carefully. She nodded along to the song lyrics and sang them confidently.

After, May Wong passed around plates of leftover cake to everyone. Nai-Nai insisted that everyone absolutely leave with exactly no less than three Tupperware containers.

I was throwing away the paper plates when Auntie Lin came to put one of the glass dishes in the sink.

I looked up. "Hi, ā-yí." I watched her expression carefully. She looked serious. Was this party okay? What if she for some reason didn't like it?

She cleared her throat. "I hear you planned all this."

I nodded. "Yeah," I said. "Kind of. Well, it was partially my idea. I was just going to bring you a cake. But Liam had the idea to make it a party. I . . ." I paused. "I just . . . didn't want you to be all by yourself on your birthday, that's all."

Her eyes were soft. Her lips pursed together, and then relaxed into a small smile. The cool breeze came in through the open window.

"I remember when your nai-nai first brought you in. Remember that? You wouldn't speak to any of us. I thought you'd be a thorn in my side all summer." She laughed. "But wah, Ruby, you sure know how to throw a good birthday party."

SIXTEEN

AFTER WEDNESDAY NIGHT'S party, Thursday was quiet. Liam played his games. Nai-Nai read. I heard Auntie Lin humming a little. But May Wong wasn't there, which was unusual for her.

"Do you think May's going to come?" I asked Liam in a hushed voice. "She usually gets here at ten on the dot."

"Yeah, it's weird that she isn't here today. You think she's at the bakery?"

I shrugged. "I don't know." My backpack was in my lap. Liam had the forms. I had sketched out a copy of a flyer that I would be making copies of over the weekend at my house. I hadn't told Nai-Nai about it. I don't know why I hadn't, really. Maybe it was Liam's and my project, and I wanted us to surprise May ourselves. Plus, Nai-Nai had a lot on her mind already. She was still thinking about Ye-Ye a lot and sometimes spent evenings going through his files. I didn't want to burden her with more.

"I'm sure she'll be here at some point," Liam said. "Wait, there's something else I wanted to talk to you about."

"What?"

Liam scooted his chair closer to the wall until we were in the corner, out of earshot. "It's about your nai-nai."

I sat up.

"I was thinking about what you'd said. Like if missing someone makes you forget things. So I brought it up to May yesterday when we were helping set up for Auntie Lin's party. She said that she was worried for your nai-nai. She said that she's known your nai-nai for close to forty years and that she hasn't seen her forget your ye-ye's name. But the other day she did."

I froze. She didn't only forget my name. She forgot Ye-Ye's.

"I thought she'd tell you today, but she isn't here. She was telling me about her aunt who was like this. She said that she had something called dementia."

"Dementia," I said slowly.

"Yeah. It starts when you forget things more than usual. It . . ." Liam shook his head. "May was talking about one of her friends at this senior center that I think your nai-nai was also friends with. Mary Hu. She had it, too."

I put my head in my hands. My forehead felt hot. I had a bad feeling, like I was starting to get sick but hadn't realized it yet. "What happens when you get dementia? What happened to Hu ā-yí?"

"I don't know," Liam said slowly. "But I've heard that when you have it . . . you keep forgetting things."

"And then? And then what?" I waited for Liam to tell me what would happen next. When it got better. But I looked at him and his face was equally as blank as mine, with none of the answers I was looking for.

"I don't know," Liam said, crestfallen. He leaned forward, his palms spread out, and I could see he was trying to make me feel better. "But your nai-nai seems mostly okay for now, Ruby. I think you just need to keep an eye on her—"

Liam kept talking, but it was as if he were shouting in a fog. I couldn't hear his words anymore. All I could think of was Nai-Nai wandering the streets of Chinatown with a blank expression on her face.

She forgot Ye-Ye's name.

I stood up. "Okay," I said, even though the world was spinning. I looked over at Nai-Nai, talking and joking with Auntie Lin. She threw her head back and laughed at something, and I felt a sense of dread. "I, um. I just need to go be with her. Right now."

"Yeah. Of course."

I stood up and walked over to where Nai-Nai was. She looked up at me and must have caught the expression on my face, because instantly her smile disappeared and she looked

186

at me with concern. "Ruby-ah? What's wrong?"

I opened my mouth but couldn't speak. Beside me, Liam looked at the ground. "I—" What could I tell her? Was it something she already knew? Was it something that she had no clue was happening? What could I say, in this senior center, right now, with everyone looking at me? Nai-Nai had seemed so happy, just a fleeting moment before. Would I ruin that?

"I'm fine," I said, trying to keep my voice steady.

"Okay," Nai-Nai said, squeezing my hand. "Nai-Nai fàngxīn." *If you're okay, I'm okay.*

She forgot Ye-Ye's name.

Just then, the door opened, and May Wong walked in.

I was still reeling from what Liam had told me about Nai-Nai and didn't catch the pointed look that Liam gave me. It was only when he reached into his laptop bag and pulled out a manila folder that I was jolted into action and stood up, holding out the flyer. But it didn't matter, anyway, because May Wong's expression was slack, her face ashen. She said, "It's done."

Nai-Nai reached out. "Oh, May," she said.

Liam asked, "What's done?"

May met our eyes. "I was meeting with Annie. We just finalized the terms of the deal with the developers."

When I spoke, my voice was rusty. "What do you mean, the terms of the deal?"

May Wong said, "We sold the bakery."

I sank back down to my seat, my stomach folding into a knot. "No," I said, and then louder, "*No.* You're not."

May looked crestfallen. "I'm sorry, Ruby. I know this isn't good news for any of us—"

"You're *not* going to do it," I said. "Tell them—tell them you're going to find another way." I frantically scooped up the flyer. "We have a plan! Liam and I. We—we put together this whole thing." I knew that Liam and I were supposed to speak about it calmly to May, like a school presentation or something, but now it was all coming out of me, rushed and scrambled.

I was aware of Nai-Nai and Auntie Lin staring at me in my periphery, their mouths open. I held up the manila folder and the papers flew out. I picked them up to show them to May. "You can apply for this thing called the Legacy Business Registry and they can help you out and—" I dropped the papers and showed her my hand-drawn flyer. "We were planning to put these up all around the neighborhood, and I was going to make a hundred copies, and—"

"Ruby, Ruby!" May Wong reached out. "Ruby, please calm down."

Shaking, I put down the flyer. "Don't you see, May? We have a *way.* You have to tell them no! You're not selling the place."

I waited for the light to come on in May Wong's eyes and for her to grab the papers like a lifeline. Instead her expression crumpled, and my heart along with it.

May said, "I have to."

"You—you said you had until the end of summer!"

"But the contract was due today." May sighed, with tears in her eyes. "We signed the papers."

My voice broke. "Tell them no. You changed your mind."

"I—I haven't," May said. "Child, I was *always* going to sell the bakery."

"No, you weren't," I said, my hands shaking. "That's not true. You said it would take something drastic. This—" I picked up the papers and held them in front of her. "This is it."

May Wong turned away from me and put her face in her hands. "It's not enough."

And I knew that was the end.

She shook her head. "You don't know the debt we've been in for the past few years. The loans Annie and I have had to take out." She looked up at me. "It's time, Ruby. I'm so sorry."

"Ruby," Auntie Lin said cautiously. "Come, sit."

I crossed my arms tightly. Sometimes I would feel something that hurt me so much and so deeply and I wouldn't know how to show how hurt I was or how to expel this furious sadness other than to let it spill out. To let it spread. Which is why I said next, "You're not sorry. We want to help and you don't want it."

I didn't register the shock on the faces of the people around me. I only saw the way May's eyes widened. She took a step backward.

She couldn't lose her bakery. We were meant to save it. It was meant to stand for decades. It had survived when others didn't. It stayed the same when the city changed.

"Think about all the people who loved your bakery," I said. "And if you sell it, they won't have that place anymore."

"Please, Ruby," May Wong said. She shook her head. "Please, stop saying this. It hurts to hear."

She had to hear it. I wanted to make sure she could hear it. "My ye-ye loved it more than anything. It was his favorite place in the world." My voice shook. "But now you're just going to *hand it over to the developers—*"

"*Enough!*" May Wong stood up, her eyes flashing. It was the first time in my life I'd heard her raise her voice. "It's *my* bakery, Ruby. You don't get to tell me how to run it."

She gathered up her bag.

Nai-Nai said, "May—"

"I'm going home," she said. "I thought I could come here to rest. But I'm not putting up with this."

And without another look, she headed for the door.

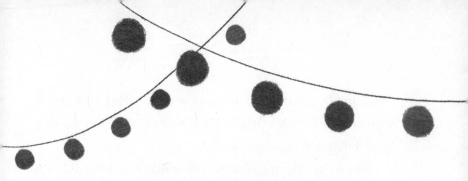

SEVENTEEN

I REALIZED, FOR the first time, that half the senior center had witnessed what had happened. I couldn't look at them.

"Ruby-ah," Nai-Nai said softly. She didn't say anything else. She just sat there and looked at me, and it was worse than if she'd scolded me.

"I'm going to get some water," I said. I walked across the room and heard voices whispering in three different dialects, probably about how much of a nuisance I was. I filled my small plastic cup and took a sip of cold machine-filtered water, trying to stop my eyes from smarting.

"Hey."

I turned around to face Liam.

"Hey," I said. "That was a disaster."

He nodded. "Yeah. Yeah. That, uh . . . was kinda hard to watch."

I leaned against the water cooler and sighed. "I know I wasn't the nicest. We just wanted to help her. But it's like she *wanted* the bakery to be sold."

I jabbed at buttons, and the water machine whirred as it spurted more cold water into my emptied cup.

"But maybe we weren't listening," Liam said softly.

I looked up. "What?"

"That's what she's been saying all along. She tried, Ruby. She's been trying for years. And maybe she just—"

"Gave up," I said sharply.

"No. Not like that," Liam said. "She decided what was best for herself. And her bakery."

"Oh," I said, getting more annoyed. I straightened up. "Cool. Great."

"What?"

"Now you're taking her side?"

"There aren't *sides* in this, Ruby! Can't you just listen for once?" Liam's voice sounded impatient. "She came in here after probably making one of the hardest decisions she's ever had to make and you decided to yell at her for it. This is *her* bakery. And as much as you or your ye-ye or your family love it, *you* can't decide what she does with it."

I took a step back and set my cup down.

"That's what I've been trying to say this whole time," Liam said. "Things change, okay? Maybe this is part of that change."

I screwed my eyes shut. Liam was always trying to see

both sides. And now, it made me furious.

This city has changed, all around, Ye-Ye said. *But this one place has stayed.*

But he was gone.

And soon, so would May's Bakery.

The place would get hollowed out. The shelves would be torn down and the small trinkets swept off those shelves. The walls would be scrubbed along with any memory of the place.

And I couldn't bear it.

Once again, the pain swelled up in me. And of course, it had to splinter around me in the worst way possible.

"You haven't even been here a year," I said bitterly. "I mean, what would you know?"

Liam stiffened. "What's *that* supposed to mean?"

"I'm sorry," I said, in a tone that meant I wasn't sorry at all. "You're new here. You wouldn't understand."

And this time, I didn't look up at him. I couldn't bring myself to.

Liam didn't say anything, and that's how I knew I hurt him, too.

"Fine," Liam finally said. "Maybe I don't. You're impossible."

He walked away. I took another sip of water and threw my cup away.

I went back and sat with Nai-Nai. She reached out and held my hand. I let her. And after a long while, when

Nai-Nai said, "That wasn't very kind to say to May," I swallowed and said, "I know."

"You should apologize to her."

"I will," I lied dully. Because if there's one person I wouldn't get mad at now, it was Nai-Nai. I watched her do crosswords the rest of the afternoon, pausing for long periods of time over the words.

Liam didn't talk to me for the rest of the day.

Nai-Nai and I had made dinner in silence. Even watching TV at night didn't bring us any joy like it would on a normal night. But it wasn't a normal night. May Wong was mad at me, and she never got mad at anyone. Liam wouldn't speak to me, and he and his grandmother had left without saying goodbye. His grandmother had shot me dirty looks as she knitted that afternoon, her needles clicking furiously.

I waited for Nai-Nai to chastise me further. But she didn't, and maybe the silence was worse. At dinner, I felt awful but I couldn't say anything, and I could barely force down the tomato-and-egg dish that Nai-Nai had made. I thought about what Liam had said about Nai-Nai's memory, before the whole thing with May happened. I watched how Nai-Nai ate and mixed her eggs and tomatoes into her rice. I observed every action, every movement, every word she would say that could give away that something was wrong with her.

She didn't say much. But it didn't matter, anyway. I now knew, without a doubt, that something was wrong.

There were a thousand thoughts swirling while we were watching our show. But the only thing I said when I turned to Nai-Nai was, "Do you remember Mary Hu?"

Nai-Nai turned to me, her eyes clear. "I do," she said softly. "She used to be good friends with May and me. But she stopped coming to the senior center."

Nai-Nai didn't say anything after that. She didn't ask why. Maybe we both knew why I'd asked. And we both didn't want to talk about it.

I couldn't sleep that night. I clutched my blankets to my chest. I turned on my phone, and then the desk lamp. The bright light hurt my eyes. I crept to the table, and, with shaking fingers, I pulled up the list where I wrote down every change that I had noticed about Nai-Nai. I curled my knees to my chest and went to my phone browser.

I wanted to kick myself for not having done this earlier, for not looking this up when the answer was at my fingertips. Maybe a part of me never wanted the answer. I laid the list flat so it was side by side with my phone. In the search bar, I typed the word in.

Dementia.

I pressed search.

Millions of results flooded the page, each with a link. *Seven stages of dementia. Five stages.*

Warning signs of Alzheimer's.

I clicked through each of them. And all the while, my chest slowly constricted. Because it was all there, with symptoms that were so clearly echoed in the handwritten list I had made.

Forgetting names of loved ones.

Forgetting common tasks and places.

Increased wandering and irritability.

Tendency to get lost in familiar places.

And it would do nothing but get worse.

If Ye-Ye were still here, he'd know what to do. He would take care of her and help her remember names and lead her home.

But Ye-Ye was gone, and Nai-Nai was alone.

It would only get worse. She would start forgetting where she had placed certain things. She would look at me and she wouldn't tell me what my name was—or would call me by the name of my mom or my aunt. She was once someone who could look at every single thing in her apartment and tell me where it came from. "I'm a mess, but an organized mess," she'd say, when Ye-Ye would gently tease her for leaving her paintbrushes or bobbins out. But now she misplaced things, and she couldn't find them anymore.

It wasn't just about forgotten objects and getting lost and foggy names. Things would fade from memory. Maybe, someday, Nai-Nai would forget who Ye-Ye was and not just his name. She'd look at me and see a stranger. Maybe it would take months. Maybe it would take five years. But

I knew that one day, she wouldn't know how to find her way home at all.

I couldn't let it go on any longer. It was serious. I had to tell Mom and Dad, and I had to do it today.

Dad was cheerful when he came to pick me up from Nai-Nai's place on Friday evening. I gave Nai-Nai an extratight hug when I went, but when I tried to say something, my throat closed up. Dad turned up NPR as we eased down the hills. He tapped on the steering wheel, but this time, it wasn't impatient tapping.

"We're stopping to pick up some takeout from Hunan House. Your mom and I are celebrating tonight. We just got our first big investment," Dad said. His eyes twinkled. "It's becoming real, Ruby. The company's set to hit all its goals this year. Isn't that exciting?"

I forced myself to say, "That's great, Dad."

He resumed his excited tapping. I opened my mouth, and then I changed my mind and chickened out. I would wait until Mom was there, too. I'd tell both of them. And Viv.

"I was just talking with Mom about how you seem happier. I knew Nai-Nai would take good care of you this summer."

I shrank back in my seat. He didn't know that Nai-Nai was forgetting names. Getting lost. Getting confused. Dad seemed too caught up in his thoughts to notice my

197

silence. We pulled into our garage.

"Ruby! You're home." Mom gave Dad a smile as he handed her the take-out boxes and my heart sank. Mom and Dad were finally happy, and I was about to make their day worse. She stopped. "Everything okay?"

"I'm going up to my room," I mumbled. "Kind of tired."

I trudged upstairs and lay on my bed, hugging my blankets to my chest. What could I say to them?

Just then, Viv burst into my room three milliseconds after knocking.

"Hey," she said, pushing her hair out of her face. "Did you happen to see my headphones anywhere when you were in my room the other day?"

She shrugged her tote bag over her shoulder. I frowned. "You're going?"

"Oh. I'm heading to a friend's birthday party. I know we were supposed to have a family dinner, but I'd had this planned for ages and Mom and Dad said it was okay." She paused. "Anyway, did you see headphones? My room's a mess, but I've been stuck in it for too long, so I thought I'd ask you to see if you happened to see them."

I turned around. "Go find them yourself."

"Really?"

"What?" My voice came out sharp, but I couldn't help it and I didn't care. She wouldn't even be here for our family dinner. "How would I know where they are? I haven't seen you in days."

Viv plopped down next to me, her eyebrows knit in annoyance. "Ruby, you okay? You seem off."

"Like you'd notice?" I snapped back. I felt awful. But now that I'd started my day like this, I couldn't turn it off, like it was becoming a big, ugly runaway storm that I couldn't control anymore.

"Are you—" Viv came around to the other side of the bed. "Are you *mad* at me for seeing my friends?"

I didn't answer her. She sat at the foot of the bed. "What's wrong?"

"I asked you if you wanted to get ice cream the other night," I said softly.

"Wait, this is what it's about? Ice cream?" Viv stood up and shrugged her bag over her shoulder. "Literally text me any day. I'm free. I mean, I guess I'm only free Saturday of next week, but, like, I'm free in the afternoon, so we should be good."

I shook my head. "It's not about *ice cream.*"

"Then *what*? Honestly, Ruby, tell me already. I have to go get ready."

And that was it. Finally, the storm burst through. "It's— I just wish you *cared* more about what was happening in this family instead of running off, that's all!"

Viv stopped. Her eyes flashed. Headstrong, stubborn Viv. "What do you *mean*, I don't care about what's happening to this family?"

I set my jaw. "You don't."

"Do you even *know* what was going on this past year?"

I sat up. "You think I don't?"

"*I* was the one trying to stop Mom and Dad from fighting all the time. And trying to talk to both Mom and Dad because they weren't talking to each other. While I was taking the hardest classes I'd ever taken and trying to sort things out between my friends and—and trying to apply to like twenty colleges and figure out what on earth I wanted to do with my life and have a halfway decent senior year." Viv threw her hands up. "And it was exhausting. So I'm *sorry* if I'm trying to live an actual life now."

She waited there for a moment. Her voice softened. "Look, I'm sorry your summer is so hard, okay? Staying with our nai-nai is probably a lot. I get it."

I didn't say anything. She was so out of touch with everything. She didn't know that getting to be with Nai-Nai was the only good thing about this summer. Now that and everything else was all falling apart, too.

"Ruby?"

I observed the paint patterns on the wall.

"Fine." I could hear her footsteps as she stormed out of the room. I curled into my blankets. I imagined myself compressing smaller and smaller, until I was denser than anything.

Last August, Scavenger Hunt Stop 6

It's a race to the top of the hill—
and down it, too.

We saw the big green house first. It was a deep leafy color, and I remembered passing it sometimes when I carpooled to soccer practice with Naomi. We'd talked about what we'd fill such a large house with. In our dream mansion, we'd build a slide that wrapped around the house and took you from the ceiling to the basement. Naomi wanted a whole floor that would be a trampoline, and we could bounce on it to other floors.

Next to the big green house was a small park, and that was where Ye-Ye and I were headed. By the time we got up the steep sidewalk, I was panting and sweat was dripping down the inside of my back. I stopped a couple of times so Ye-Ye could catch up. "Lǎo-le," Ye-Ye said. *I'm old.* "I used to run up these hills ten times a day in high school, you know that?"

"Ten times?" I let my jacket fall so that it looped around my shoulders.

"Yeah," Ye-Ye said. "I was an active kid."

"Speaking of running," I said. "You said there was some kind of race?" I looked around. The paths were wide and winding, looping around, but they weren't very long. "We're not . . ."

"Oh, not *us*," Ye-Ye said. He sat down on a bench and reached into his bag for something and pulled it out.

In his hand were two Hot Wheels cars.

My eyes widened. "Ye-Ye, I'm *twelve*."

"Well, I'm seventy and I still think it's fun," Ye-Ye said. His voice was mild, but I could tell he was a little hurt. "I always liked to race cars downhill with your dad when he was a kid. But we can just sit and rest, if you'd like."

Suddenly I felt bad. Sure, I would never do this with Naomi and Mia. But they weren't here, and besides, Ye-Ye always had one silly thing or another up his sleeve. "I pick the one with the flames on the side," I said, trying to smooth things over. "That one's always faster."

We lined our cars up at the sidewalk. I pulled mine back, just a little bit so I heard the click.

"Finish line is at the next bench," Ye-Ye said.

I said, "Ready—"

"Go!" Ye-Ye said, and we let them go at the same time. We crouched close to the ground as the little cars hurtled off, bumping their way down the path.

"Flames is winning right now," I said, as the cars skittered downhill.

"Hold on," Ye-Ye said. "I'm not calling anything just yet."

Just then, the path before the cars tilted forward and the blue car pitched into mine.

"Hey!" I sprang to my feet. "Did you see—"

The car with the flames teetered off the path and then into the bushes that lined the side of the path.

"I win," Ye-Ye said. "All it takes is some experience."

"That's *all* luck," I said. I marched down to the end of the path, where I scooped up both cars. "We're racing again."

I tried it all—sending the car off at an angle, sending the car off slowly so it could build momentum—but Ye-Ye always had some trick I didn't know about. I finally beat him on the fourth run, when his car stumbled into a small rock and flipped over.

"Okay, tell me how Dad did it."

"He always tried to go for the path of least resistance," Ye-Ye said. "Whatever he did, the car didn't flip over. He was always careful like that. You like to go fast."

I leaned back and sighed. "Yeah, that's what Dad says, too. He says Viv and I rush into things too quickly."

"Your dad is careful," Ye-Ye said. "Sometimes too careful."

"What was he like in middle school?" I leaned back on the bench, cradling my car in my hands. "Was he . . . cool?"

Ye-Ye tipped his head back and laughed. "Not really."

"No?"

"He was, well . . . bookish," Ye-Ye said with a small conspiratorial smile. "Imagine a skinny kid with the largest Coke-bottle glasses you've ever seen."

"Dad was a big nerd?" I couldn't imagine it now.

"Yeah, he took a while to grow into himself, I think,"

Ye-Ye said. "He didn't get his first girlfriend until college. And when he brought her to meet us, he went to the bathroom so many times during dinner that Nai-Nai thought she had given him something bad to eat. But really, he was just in there rehearsing what to say to her."

I laughed at the thought. "But that girlfriend was . . ."

"Your mother," Ye-Ye said. "It worked out, after all."

I turned the toy car over in my hands. I thought about telling Ye-Ye about the silence in our house now that Mom and Dad weren't talking to each other anymore. I'd seen Mom's and Dad's eyes light up when they looked at each other, back when I was little, but now they stayed up yelling words across a living room. Maybe Ye-Ye already knew, but I didn't want to tell him if he didn't.

Instead, I just scooped up Ye-Ye's car. I understood why this was kind of fun now. "Let's race again," I said to Ye-Ye. "Just one last time. I promise."

"If you say so," Ye-Ye said.

And this time, I was determined to win.

EIGHTEEN

MOM AND DAD spooned the takeout onto our fancy plates and reheated them in the microwave. They set them all nice in the center of the dinner table. "There's pistachio ice cream for dessert," Mom said. "In the freezer."

I could barely smile. All throughout dinner, the food kept getting stuck in my throat. I tried to force the stir-fried beef down, but I could barely swallow.

"I told you," Mom said. "Hiring Ethan was a good idea."

Dad grabbed Mom's hand and squeezed it. "You give good advice. And now that we closed on our first round, we can finally relax for a bit."

Mom grinned, and then turned to me. She scooped a spoonful of stir-fried bell peppers onto my plate. "Veggies, Ruby. Don't forget."

I poked at them.

Mom asked, "You feeling okay, Ruby? You look sick."

I put my chopsticks down. Mom and Dad were happy. For once. A year ago, I didn't think we'd have a dinner like this again. I wanted it to go on. I wanted to eat my pistachio ice cream and not worry about anything. But I put my chopsticks down. "I need to talk to you guys about something."

Mom sat down in her seat. Dad looked up from his food.

"I'm worried about Nai-Nai."

Dad said slowly, "What do you mean?"

"She's—she's forgetting things," I said. My voice was quiet. "She's forgetting names. She forgot my name. Ye-Ye's name. She called me Jeanie the other day. And sometimes—" I took a deep breath. "Sometimes she keeps mixing up the things in her kitchen. She'll put things in the wrong place." I said, "I think she has something called dementia."

Dad put down his fork. He asked, slowly, "How long has she been forgetting things?"

"I don't know. For weeks, now."

"The older you get, the more likely you are to forget things," Dad said.

"But this isn't normal," I said. "She wouldn't forget Ye-Ye's name."

Dad put his face in his hands. He slumped into his seat.

"Is there anything else that is going on?" Mom said. "Is Nai-Nai just forgetting names?"

I steadied my palms under the table. I had to say it.

"A few weeks ago on a Thursday I . . . went to Naomi's birthday sleepover."

Mom stiffened.

I tried to keep my voice steady. "Nai-Nai agreed to come with me and drop me off at her house and pick me up in the morning. But in the morning Nai-Nai wasn't there. And so I took the Muni to Nai-Nai's place and she was lost. She said she was heading to the station but she wasn't anywhere near it. She was going to May's. I don't know what to do. I didn't want to come talk to you until I knew for sure something was wrong. But now I'm sure." I shook my head. "Something isn't right. Nai-Nai shouldn't be getting lost around her own home. If—" My voice caught in my throat. "If she has dementia, it's only going to get worse."

Both my parents' eyebrows were knit. Mom and Dad exchanged a look.

"Ruby," Dad said. "You went to your friend's sleepover?"

"I know I shouldn't have gone," I said. "But Nai-Nai agreed to it and I hadn't talked to Naomi in—"

"Honestly, Ruby, how irresponsible could you be?" Mom's voice rose. "Going to a friend's house? Without telling us? Or asking us?"

"You wouldn't have said yes!"

"That's beside the point! You were supposed to stay and have your nai-nai look after you, not do things behind our back. And *especially* if things aren't okay for her. And you couldn't even do that." Mom pressed her fingertips to her temples. "Ruby, tiān-nah, why are you always such a—a *headache* for us?"

My eyes started smarting.

"You should have told us this right when it happened," Dad said. "You shouldn't have kept this from us."

"I'm sorry," I whispered, trying to keep my voice from breaking. "But I didn't know—"

"Are you full?" Dad asked.

"What? I'm not hungry," I said. "I just want to talk about Nai-Nai."

"Then go upstairs."

"What are you going to do about Nai-Nai?"

"That's for us to discuss," Mom said. "As adults."

"Come on, Ruby," Dad said. "This conversation is over. Go upstairs."

Slowly, I stood up. I pushed in my chair and the legs made a hollow, scraping sound. As I climbed the stairs, I heard Mom say under her breath, "That child."

I went into my room and leaned against the door.

I shouldn't have gone to the sleepover. I knew that, ten times over. If only I hadn't gone, Nai-Nai wouldn't have gotten lost and then—

This still would have happened. Nai-Nai still would have forgotten things.

Maybe Mom was right. Maybe I should have told them sooner. I leaned against the wall. And after a while, I opened my door, straining to hear them talk in their hushed adult voices.

"It sounds serious," Mom was saying. "From what Ruby is telling us. If she really is forgetting where places are." I heard Mom sigh. "She's having a hard year."

Dad said softly, "I know."

"If it really is dementia or Alzheimer's . . ."

Dad was quiet for a moment. "I know."

"This can't be good."

And this time, Dad didn't say anything.

Mom said, "What should we do?"

I heard Dad exhale. He was quiet for a long time. "She lives alone in the apartment. That's what I'm most worried about."

"So what you're saying is . . . ?"

"There are full-time care facilities. Maybe she needs a nurse or something to take care of her."

"Now?"

"At some point. But we need to schedule an appointment for her immediately."

I leaned against the wall, my heart constricting.

They were going to put Nai-Nai in a retirement home. They were going to send her away.

What had I *done*?

When I went downstairs to get breakfast the next morning, Mom was having coffee in the kitchen.

I went into the pantry and took a Pop-Tart. Mom gave me a look. "I toasted some whole wheat bread over here."

How was she so calm? I opened the Pop-Tart wrapper and took a bite.

Mom glanced at her watch. "Vivian should be coming back," she said, to the phone.

"She just texted me," Dad said through the phone speaker. "Oh, by the way, we should switch the composting."

"Are you putting Nai-Nai in a senior home?" I blurted out.

Dad went silent over the speaker.

Mom looked at the screen. "I'm going to call you back in a bit." And then she put her phone down and looked at me.

"We're still talking about it," Mom said. "We're trying to figure it out between us right now. We're going to get your nai-nai in for some evaluations, and then—"

"You can't," I said, my voice shaking. I thought of Nai-Nai in a room with white walls and no TV, far from her home. Silent. Just like they'd done to Hu ā-yí. "You can't take her away from her home."

Mom put her coffee down. "This is between your dad and me. You've done enough."

I stood up. "Fine. Then I'm going." I whirled around and stuffed my Pop-Tart into my pocket. I took my hoodie from the sofa and marched toward the door.

"Where are you going?"

I turned around to face Mom. "I'm going."

"Ruby Chu! First the sleepover, now this? You can't—"

"I'm going to *Nai-Nai's*," I said. "Isn't that what you wanted for me all this summer? To be with Nai-Nai? Well, I'm going there."

Mom's face turned red. "But your dad has the car!"

"I'll take the train." I put my phone in the pocket of my hoodie and heard the door close behind me.

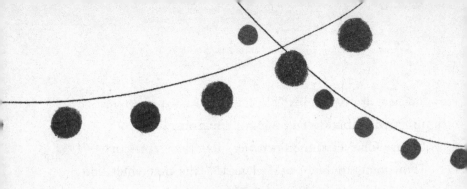

NINETEEN

I HAD TO be there for Nai-Nai.

I ran down the street to the Muni station. I walked down the stairs. Head down, eyes trained on my shoes. With shaking fingers, I put money in the machine for a ticket.

Dad would be furious when Mom told him what I did. I could already picture the steely look in his eyes. *That child,* Mom would sigh, again. *Why can't you do anything right?*

Why are you always a headache for us?

I held my head in my hands, as if I could shake out all of my thoughts.

Why did you go to Naomi's that day?

Why did I bother trying in the first place? Why did I try to patch things up with Naomi? Why did I keep reaching out to my sister when she didn't want to be around the house anymore? And *why* did I take it upon myself to try to save May Wong's bakery? Every time I tried to do something, it would backfire in my face. And all I did was cause problems. For everyone in my life.

The train roared past us. I glanced at the timetable. The next train was mine. The N line.

All I did was make things worse. I thought of May's furious expression as she turned away from me that day. And then Liam, finally, looking me in the eye and saying, *you're impossible.*

The train screeched to a stop in front of me, the wind gusting up from the tracks. I stepped in and took a seat on one of the hard chairs. I leaned back against the window.

Why couldn't I do a single thing right?

And *why* couldn't I move on from Ye-Ye's death?

If I'd only stayed thirty minutes longer, I thought. *If only I didn't leave. If only I'd known what was happening. If only I'd gone to find Nai-Nai. If only—*

If only I'd saved him.

He'd be here with me.

The train hurtled to the next stop, and then to the next, and I glanced around. The subway car was pretty empty. Two teenagers sat in the back, one leaning on another's shoulder. Someone was reading in the corner. I pulled out my phone. Mom's messages flooded the screen. I glanced through them all and barely read the words.

I typed back, **i'm going to be staying at nai-nai's for the weekend.**

I set my phone down next to me, and I closed my eyes and leaned back.

I'd spend the day at Nai-Nai's place. I would help her make noodles and tea in her sunlit kitchen. I'd reorganize the spice rack. We would sit on the couch and watch Chinese dramas. If she forgot a name, I'd remind her.

Even if I had done everything else wrong, I could still be there for her.

I walked out of the Muni station and ran to Nai-Nai's building. I took the stairs by two and before I knew it, I was knocking on the door of apartment 3B. "Nai-Nai, it's me."

I waited there for a moment, fidgeting with my sleeves. I heard the shuffling of footsteps, a pause, and then the turn of the doorknob. I expected to see Nai-Nai in her flowery pants, shrugging a sweater around her and fluffing up her hair.

Instead I met a frazzled Nai-Nai who was tugging a jacket around her and carrying a backpack in her hands. Her hair was wild and she wore bright shirts haphazardly layered over one another and flowery pants. Her wide eyes darted from side to side around me. She reached out and pulled me into the apartment.

"Nai-Nai?"

"Ruby," she said. "They're going to send me away."

My heart dropped into my stomach. "What?"

So she knew, then.

She looked up at me, her jaw set. "They're going to put

me into a home. Just like Mary Hu's family did with her. That's what they're going to do, aren't they?"

"I—" I stopped. How did *she* know? "I don't know."

"Your ba called this morning," she said. She paced in circles, putting down her jacket on the couch, then picking it up again. "He told me that they want me to see a doctor. That's what happened to Mary. The doctor told her family to put her in a nursing home. So they did. You can't let them do this to me."

I squeezed my eyes shut. Nai-Nai needed help.

"They're worried about you," I said, trying to keep a collected voice. "*I'm* worried. We don't know if you can take care of yourself anymore."

"Take care!" She whirled around, her eyes wild. "I know Chinatown more than I know anything. I've lived in this apartment for twenty years. I lived down the street for twenty more. I raised a *family*. Your ba grew up here."

I shook my head. "They're just talking about it right now. They're not going to—"

"They will," Nai-Nai said. I steadied her by her shoulders. She folded into me, and I pulled her in, breathing in the scent of lavender and powder and hundred-flower oil. I could feel her shaking.

"I lost him," Nai-Nai said against my shoulder, her voice breaking. "I can't lose this home, too." She broke away and grabbed me by the hands. "Ruby, you should go back home."

"No! I'm not going home. I'm staying here with you."

"But I'm not staying. I have to go." She turned around and started putting things into her backpack. A map. A plastic water bottle. Snacks from the pantry.

"Nai-Nai," I said slowly. "What are you doing?"

"They're coming to take me away," Nai-Nai said. "They're planning on taking me away from this place. So I'm going."

"No, Nai-Nai," I said. "They're *not taking you*."

But Nai-Nai seemed like she was in her own world. She shook her head and put more snacks into her backpack. I stumbled back, helplessly surveying the situation. What could I have done? What could I do now? Mom and Dad needed to know what was going on. But to Nai-Nai, help meant that they were going to take her away, which made me feel even worse.

I had to keep her calm. I asked, "Where are you going?"

She whirled around to face me. "I'm going where they can't find me."

What did that even mean?

Nai-Nai looked around her. And she slowly slung her backpack over her shoulder.

"Nai-Nai—"

"Don't try to stop me, Ruby," she said. "I'm going whether you want me to or not. I can't let them put me in a nursing home. You understand? I *can't*."

Her voice was forceful, but I could hear the tremble.

Nai-Nai felt lost. Abandoned. I knew what she was feeling, then. Like no one else was looking out for her. Like everything in front of her was hopeless, and the best thing to do was to run away.

I had to be there for her. And that meant being with her, for everything. I couldn't let her wander by herself. I took a deep breath, trying to keep my voice steady. "I won't. Nai-Nai, I won't leave you."

She looked me in the eye.

"I'm not trying to stop you." I straightened up carefully. In my mind I sketched a plan. I would walk around with her enough to keep her calm. I'd talk her out of her panic, and I'd bring her home. I'd show her that I was there, that Mom and Dad weren't planning on taking her away, that she had me. But that meant going along with what she was doing. "I'm coming with you."

TWENTY

WHEN I WAS little and got mad at Mom and Dad, like really mad, I would climb into the family walk-in closet at the top of the stairs right next to my room. I'd fold myself into the dry-cleaned clothes and think about running away. I thought about sailing the bay and into the Pacific Ocean. I thought about taking the Caltrain and going south. But I never thought about it for more than five minutes. And when I was done being mad, I'd take a deep breath and climb out of the closet.

I never thought I would actually run away.

And I never thought I'd be doing it with my grandmother.

You're not running away, my mind protested. *You're just going to take Nai-Nai around the block. You're going to calm her down. And when she is calm enough, she'll go home.*

I made two rules. I'd always keep Nai-Nai in sight. And I'd get her home by noon. Afternoon at the latest.

Nai-Nai didn't tell me where we were going, but she was walking fast enough for me to take longer steps to keep up with her. We walked past the fresh vegetable market, but Nai-Nai didn't stop at any of the stands. We passed by the pharmacy and a bookshop and turned on a road, and then another that looked familiar somehow. I'd lost count of the blocks we'd walked when Nai-Nai finally slowed and turned around. "Are you hungry?"

I shook my head. "Are you?"

"No. I was wondering if you were. Because I brought snacks."

"It's okay, Nai-Nai. I'm not hungry now."

She paused. "Where do you want to go?"

I stopped. "Are we . . . not going somewhere?"

"We can go anywhere we want," Nai-Nai said. She grinned. "We're free. No one can tell us what to do."

I looked back down the street. Sure, Nai-Nai was scatterbrained and free-spirited, but she was never like this. I tried, tentatively, to say, "Let's go home, Nai-Nai."

She was stubborn. "I asked you where you wanted to go. I didn't ask if you thought I should go home."

I sighed. "They're not going to put you in a nursing home."

"They will. Your ba said they were thinking about it."

"*Thinking about it*," I said.

"Which means they will."

I sighed.

"Are you hungry?"

"You just asked that."

"Did I?"

"I'm going to pull up some place we can go to on my maps." I took out a Pop-Tart and a wad of paper that I'd stashed in my backpack. I rooted around for my phone and came up with nothing.

"Nai-Nai," I said. "Did I leave my phone at your place?"

She didn't answer. I tried to think of the last place I had it. I had it in the morning, and then I carried it with me to the Muni, and then I—

I'd left it next to me. On the subway.

My phone was gone.

Panic surged up in me. *Oh, no, no, no.* Mom and Dad were going to be furious. I started hyperventilating. Maybe I could go back to the same train. Maybe I could track down the car I was in—

"Ruby? Ruby? Are you okay?" Nai-Nai reached for me.

I tried to calm down. If I freaked out, Nai-Nai would, too. It was my job to keep her calm. I would get her home and then deal with the phone thing. Maybe I could call the train line from Nai-Nai's home phone. Maybe someone had turned it in. "I'm okay. Nai-Nai, we should go home."

"No. We can't."

When Nai-Nai had an idea, she was stubborn as an ox. There was no point talking in circles. It was impossible to reason with her. We stood there for a moment. I stayed and looked around, desperately.

We had to do *something*.

Come to think of it, there *was* something familiar about the blue house on the corner, the way the trees lined up on the gently sloping street. "We're on Green," I said. I ran to the corner, where Green met Hyde Street.

In the little house that hides on green, make a trade and stay awhile.

A strange chill washed over me. Suddenly I was rooted to the street. Suddenly it was a year ago, and I was puzzling over the clues on a piece of paper. And suddenly I wasn't just thinking of Nai-Nai, but of something that Ye-Ye had left behind.

"I need to see something," I said. I whirled around.

"Finally," Nai-Nai sighed. "We have somewhere to go."

"It's not a place," I said. "It's a house. A little house. A—" I saw it at the end of the street. "A library."

"A library? Out of all the places, you choose a library?" Nai-Nai shrugged. "Okay, let's go."

"It's not any library," I said. "It was one of Ye-Ye's stops last year. One of those Little Free Libraries. You bring a book in and then you take a book. And Ye-Ye brought this book in." I could see the little wooden house at the end of the street now, the blue cottage with white windowsills and

221

painted flowers blooming up its walls. "I just want to see if it's still there."

"Let's go find it, then," Nai-Nai said, and relief filled me. At least there would be a purpose to our walk now. We'd check on the Little Free Library, and we could go home, and then I'd search for my phone.

"It's there," I said. "I just know it is."

Nai-Nai stopped in front of the Little Free Library. She pointed. "Here?"

I sucked in a breath and opened the door.

I scanned the shelves. I flipped through the spines, feeling the flimsy cover paper. Maybe it was hidden under a big cookbook. Maybe it was tucked behind a book. Maybe it was in the corner. Maybe—

No, no, no.

I took books out and scoured the shelves.

I stepped back. "It's gone," I said softly. My words felt hollow. Of course someone would have taken it. It had been almost a year since I followed the clue down to this street.

French Cooking with Julia Child was still there.

How to Invest in Real Estate was still there.

But Ye-Ye's book wasn't.

"Ruby-ah," Nai-Nai said.

I shook my head. "That's okay," I said. "It's a free library. Someone was bound to take it."

"Was it a good book? Did you want it back?"

"It wasn't the *book*," I said. I could picture the book so

clearly in my mind. A picture of gold trees and mountains. *To the next wonderful stranger who decides to pick this book up. Happy trails.* "It was—" I stopped. "It was *his* book."

How long did the book stay in there? Was it taken the day we left it? Did it stand for months in the blue shelves? I guess it didn't matter anymore. It was gone, and so was every trace that Ye-Ye and I were here.

"It was the first official stop on the scavenger hunt last year," I said softly. "After we went to May's."

"Oh," Nai-Nai said wistfully. Her eyes met mine. "What was the clue?"

"In the little house that hides on green, make a trade and stay awhile." My throat felt thick. "Because it was a little house. On the corner of Hyde and Green."

"That clever one, your ye-ye." Nai-Nai turned to me. "Where was the next stop?"

"The stationery shop in Japantown. He took me there to look at fun erasers."

"The one across from the gardening shop?"

"Yeah," I said. "That one."

"Let's go," Nai-Nai said.

"Wait," I said. "To the stationery store?"

She had a small smile. "That's the next stop, isn't it?"

Bright colors spun around us, swirling up toward the ceiling. It was just like I remembered it. Back when we were in the eraser shop, Nai-Nai peered at the shelves curiously, but here, Nai-Nai looked around in wonder, in her element. "You said this is where you got the purple satin from?"

"Yep," I said. "It was the one that looked so soft and shiny, like water."

"Oh, I remember," Nai-Nai said. "I made a fancy party dress out of it."

"You did?"

"I didn't know what I was making it for. I thought I'd make a prom dress for Vivian, but it didn't really turn out that way because I added these cap sleeves. And then I thought, maybe I'd wear it to some fancy dinner party." She chuckled. "Ai-yah, as if I have many fancy dinner parties to go to."

"We can host one," I said.

Nai-Nai tilted her head.

"We threw a birthday party, didn't we?" I smiled. "Who says we can't host a fancy dinner party?"

"I'd wear my purple dress," Nai-Nai said. "And I can give you one of my dresses to wear. There's one I made with sunflowers."

"I'd love that," I said.

"I could bring out my clay tea set. From Hangzhou."

"And everyone is invited," I said. "Even Auntie Lin's cats can come."

"Only if they dress up!" Nai-Nai giggled, and I laughed with her, because it was ridiculous and funny to think of Auntie Lin's cats in bow ties.

A heavy feeling settled in my stomach. "Nai-Nai, do you think May is mad at me?"

Nai-Nai looked at me plainly. "You know it's been a hard time for her."

I nodded. The more I remembered the words I said to her, the worse I felt. "I just wanted to help."

"I know," Nai-Nai said. "Child, I know."

We wandered farther into the store, past the bolts of fabric sprawled out on the table and the ribbons and toward the wall of velvet. We leaned against the wall. After a morning of walking around a little library and a Japanese stationery shop, it felt good to lean. I tucked my jacket into my bag and realized that my phone was still missing, but I pressed down that worry. The most important thing was that Nai-Nai was calming down. I'd deal with the phone later.

"Ye-Ye told me a story here," I said.

Nai-Nai looked over. "He did?"

"He told me the story of how you two met."

Nai-Nai's voice softened. "And how did he tell it?"

I watched a piece of tulle drift in the fan breeze. "He says that you worked at a coffee shop in New York. And that he came in all the time because he wanted to talk to you."

"Ah," Nai-Nai said. "I didn't know how someone could like bad coffee so much."

"He liked you, Nai-Nai."

"Oh, I knew."

"You knew?"

"I eventually figured out he didn't like the coffee." Her eyes twinkled.

"He says you showed him around New York."

"Oh, yes. There was this one noodle place. I went there all the time. The . . ." Nai-Nai's eyes clouded. "I can't remember anymore. But it was on the corner of that street with the Laundromat and the photo shop. I took him all around the city, you know. I just didn't introduce him to my family."

"Why didn't you?"

"In the times back then," Nai-Nai said, "you didn't bring a boy home unless you were sure you were going to marry him."

"Were you sure?"

"My family wanted me to marry someone from a Hangzhou family. They had their sights set on someone else. Your ye-ye also never told me his feelings. And then he suddenly left New York to take care of his mother and I thought—maybe we were meant to stay in our cities. Maybe it wasn't really meant to be anything more than a friendship."

"And then?"

"And that was that," Nai-Nai said, twirling a red ribbon around her finger. "But I always remembered him. Sometimes I thought about flying across the country just to see him. But that wasn't very practical. It would be too late. He probably married someone else by then. But then—my friend moved to San Francisco. And she wanted me to visit. And I—I can't explain it, but I felt like there was a thread, pulling me."

"So you went."

"I did. And I was having lunch with my friend at this place and I looked across the street, and there was this roast duck shop. Right next to it, people were lined up around the block for the bakery. I remember your ye-ye telling me about this roast duck shop and this bakery, so I pulled my friend to go to the bakery that afternoon. I met May and had the most delicious egg tarts I'd ever tasted. I told her I knew someone in New York who talked about her bakery all the time, and then next thing I knew, she phoned up your ye-ye and he came to meet me."

"And then he told you he liked you!"

"Not yet," Nai-Nai said. "But he did ask me to stay and walk around the city."

"So he showed you around."

"He took me everywhere. He took me to the sea and to this ice cream place we loved. He took me up and down the streets and to this park where you could look over the whole city." She glanced over. "Those became my scavenger hunt spots."

"*You* had a scavenger hunt, too?"

Nai-Nai's cheeks turned pink with joy. "Of course. This one I went on alone, three months after I moved to San Francisco and nine months after I visited my friend. He put clues to each of the locations. Right when I climbed all the way to the top of the park, your ye-ye was waiting with a ring."

"And you married him!" I said, bouncing. "Wait. So what happened to the Hangzhou guy your parents liked?"

Nai-Nai looked at me. "Does this really need to be a sixty-part Chinese drama? I'm here, aren't I?"

"Tell me more about living by the beach."

We now sat at the park next to the green house. I pointed out the path where Ye-Ye and I raced cars last year. But Nai-Nai and I didn't have any Hot Wheels at the ready, and besides, our feet were tired, and we'd walked plenty, to the square where Ye-Ye and I played go and then to here.

So we sat and looked over the city. Nai-Nai held up a small circular package. I beamed. "Haw flakes!"

"Want some?" She tore the package and took a piece of candy. I took a piece. My lips puckered at the tangy sweetness. We ate the snacks that she had packed, after all.

"The beach," Nai-Nai said, leaning back. "Sara ā-yí lived by the beach." It was the wrong name again, but I didn't say anything. "She had a little cottage. Her husband passed a few years ago, so it was just her, living by the sea. She woke up at five o'clock every single morning and did her arm and leg exercises. And then she dragged me out of bed to do the exercises with her. At first I hated it. I just wanted to stay in bed all day and stare at the ceiling. And it was cold in the mornings. But she wouldn't hear it. She told me I was worse at getting up than when her boys were teenagers. She pulled me out of the bed and we did those exercises by the sea. We must have looked ridiculous to the surfer boys who came by while we were swinging our arms and legs about in the background, bundled up in five layers."

I smiled at the thought of Nai-Nai and her flower pants upstaging surfer dudes.

"But somehow, she was right. I did feel better."

"What would you do the rest of the day?"

"We'd sit. She had a little garden in her backyard and worked in it. Sometimes, she drove me around. We talked a lot. Sometimes, I'd go to the beach by myself."

"Why by yourself?"

"Because I wanted to. I'd watch the waves for hours. Sometimes I'd talk to him."

"You heard Ye-Ye?"

"I'd just talk," Nai-Nai said. "I'd talk to the sea, and I'd imagine him answering in my mind. I imagined what it would be like if we lived in a cottage by the sea. We were going to, once."

"You were?"

"I wanted to do that after we both retired," Nai-Nai said. "But your ye-ye wanted to stay. And then Vivian was born, and then you. And we wanted to stay near. But that little dream always lived in the back of my mind."

I said softly, "I'd live in a beach cottage with you."

"Ruby-ah," Nai-Nai said. "That's kind of you."

"No, I really *would*," I said. "Just you and me. We'd see the ocean and make tea in the mornings and watch dramas at night. And we can get you a sewing machine so you can make all the fancy dresses you want and get you a painting set so we can paint pictures of the ocean. And—" I stopped, and my words felt thick in my throat, because the more I thought about it, the more I wanted it.

No more hard classes. No more sitting alone at the lunch table.

"And we can host fancy dinner parties every week," Nai-Nai said. "And we can put up lights around the porch. And everyone has to dress up and dance on the beach." She laughed, and her laugh was a beautiful sound.

I said quietly, "I wish you'd taken me with you."

Nai-Nai looked at me gently. "Your family would have missed you."

"They don't care." My eyes filled with tears. "My mom and dad think that all I do is cause problems. My sister barely talks to me anymore."

"You know they love you."

"Not the way you and Ye-Ye loved me."

"They're trying their best," Nai-Nai said. "Child, I promise."

"If they love me, then they love you, too," I said. "They want to help you."

Nai-Nai looked ahead for a long moment. She nodded. And then she turned to me. "Where did you go from here?"

"There is one more stop," I said. "I don't know if it's there anymore. But we can try and see."

Last August, Scavenger Hunt Stop 7

Up by the sea in the stone fort with the trees,
come plant some things to bloom and feed.

I set down the clue. "Stone fort," I said slowly. I tried to think of all the places I knew. "Is there a stone fort in the city?"

"It's the last stop," Ye-Ye said. "I'm sure you'll figure this one out. Although a map might help."

I retrieved the map from my backpack and patted it down between us. "Is it to the south?"

"North," Ye-Ye said.

"By the sea," I said. "Got it." I shifted up, scanning the piers and—

"Fort Mason is the first fort I see," I said. "Wait a minute." *Stone fort.* I looked up. "Fort Mason?"

His smile made the corners of his eyes crinkle. "I knew you'd figure it out."

"Come plant some things to bloom and feed." I stared at the last half of the clue. "What are we planting?"

"That's still a secret for a bit." Ye-Ye stood from the park bench. I stood with him and collected the Hot Wheels cars. I wiggled my toes in my shoes. The bottoms of my feet were beginning to ache. As if he could read my mind, Ye-Ye said, "Let's take the bus at the end of the street. Let your ye-ye rest his knees."

I leaned against the window, letting the afternoon sun warm my cheeks. A bit of hunger began to gnaw at the pit of my stomach. I started to think about what would be for dinner. Maybe Ye-Ye would get something from May's again on the way back. I was still craving a char siu bun, even though I'd stuffed myself earlier in the day. Or maybe Nai-Nai would be making her beef-noodle soup tonight. My mouth watered while I daydreamed about the rich broth and the thick noodles.

"We're here, Ruby."

The bus creaked to a stop, and Ye-Ye and I got off. We walked into the park, and in the distance, we could see the hills sloping into the blue of the bay. "Just a little farther," Ye-Ye said. And after we passed some cars, Ye-Ye stopped in front of the open gate.

I peered through. "It's a big garden," I said.

"The community garden."

I turned around, my eyes wide. "You and Nai-Nai got off the waitlist?"

Ye-Ye grinned. "I did."

"That means—"

"I finally get to plant my own garden."

"You were going to plant tomatoes and cucumbers," I remembered. He told me all about it years ago. San Francisco was a city, which meant things didn't have much space to grow, except for buildings. It had been his dream to get a little patch of land in this community garden that overlooked the bay and the Golden Gate Bridge.

"Someday," he said. "I will." He turned. "Want to see my plot?"

He led me through the open gate, and I looked around in wonder. We were surrounded by green all around. Vines climbed high on trellises. I could see pea plants beginning to flower, tender stalks beginning to sprout through the soil, and lilies opening up to the sun. I passed by someone's garden, and their hydrangeas brushed my arm.

Finally, we got to Ye-Ye's garden plot.

"Are we planting your vegetables today? Tomatoes and cucumbers?"

"Well," he said. "I was thinking we could plant something else here first. Remember our fifth stop last year in the science museum?"

"The butterfly exhibit," I said. "It was my favorite."

"You told me all about your science project with your friends. And it got me thinking."

He handed me an envelope. I opened it carefully and shook out a packet of seeds.

He smiled. "How about we plant a butterfly garden?"

TWENTY-ONE

MY HEART NOW hammered in my chest when Nai-Nai and I got off the bus. Nai-Nai looked around. "This is the stop?"

"It's farther in," I said. "This way."

I took Nai-Nai down the sidewalk. In the clear view of the street, we could look over the tops of houses and see where the skyline met the blue of the bay. In the grassy area palm trees swayed in the wind. I led her down a small path and, finally, to the garden gate, surrounded by trees and vines.

"It's a garden," Nai-Nai said.

"Did Ye-Ye ever show you?"

"He only told me he got a garden somewhere in the city," she said. "He told me he'd show me after things grew in it."

"This was the last stop," I said.

I paused at the gate and took a deep breath. Ye-Ye's garden was around the corner, just out of sight. I remembered kneeling over the fresh dirt, planting the tiny seeds and patting soft dirt over them. "Milkweeds and daisies and wallflowers," I read from the list on the back of Ye-Ye's envelope. "Aster, wild sunflower, prairie clover . . ." I looked up at Ye-Ye. "Will the butterflies really come?"

"If we take care of the garden," Ye-Ye said. "We can come back every month to water the seeds."

Now I squeezed my eyes shut. It had been over seven months since I'd been here. Six months since Ye-Ye collapsed in his apartment and my family rushed to the hospital, only for the doctor to tell us it had been too late to save him. And I'd forgotten about this. What if the garden was overrun by weeds? What if nothing sprouted? What if it was like the Little Free Library all over again?

I should have come back to check. I should have visited.

"Ruby?"

I opened my eyes. I needed to see it for myself. "Let's go in."

I slowly led Nai-Nai through the gate. I walked in, bracing myself for an empty garden plot, the dirt still as we left it. We made our way down, past the broad leaves and tall vines of the other gardens, and then we rounded the corner.

And I stopped.

"Oh," I said, in wonder.

Because it was still all there. And it wasn't just *there*. Wildflowers reached toward the sun, twining with the bright daisies and the purple bergamot and the milkweed, sprouting every which way. The afternoon light touched the petals, turning them into a burst of color.

"Look," Nai-Nai said in a hushed voice.

There, perched at the top of the tallest flower, was a monarch butterfly.

"It's all *here*," I whispered. And my throat felt tight and tears came to my eyes. I met Nai-Nai's eyes, and we looked at the flowers together. My feet were sore. My legs ached. All these scavenger-hunt stops, and it was as if we were still searching for him in a city that was once his home. Six stops over the city, and we couldn't find anything.

But now at once I breathed in the soft scents of the flowers and suddenly it was as if Ye-Ye were right next to us, again, with his laugh and his light steps and his wonder and joy, folding the seeds into my hands. His garden was here all along, blooming and beautiful. And so was he.

"Piào-liàng," Nai-Nai said. *Beautiful.* She reached a hand toward the butterfly, but then stopped.

The butterfly's wings folded, slowly. And after a heartbeat, the sun's rays changed, and it was gone. Nai-Nai looked at me. "Did you see—"

I nodded.

"Ah," Nai-Nai said. "Guess he just wanted to say hello."

I looked up. *Hi, Ye-Ye.*

We stood for a long moment in the garden, just the two of us. Nai-Nai looked at the flowers, lightly setting her fingertip on the petals. "So many colors. The butterflies must be happy."

"He used to tell me that he wanted a tomato garden, but then two years ago one of the stops was a butterfly exhibit. I guess he really liked it."

"He remembers," Nai-Nai said. "You tell him you like something once, and he'd remember it for the rest of his life." Nai-Nai straightened up and looked at the sky. "Looks like he remembers to water these flowers, too."

I laughed. I thought of all the times it had rained in the winter, when I would jump out of the way when car tires splashed puddles onto the sidewalk. "I'll come back every month," I said, my throat tight. "I'll remember to water them."

We stood there for a while more.

"My knees are tired," Nai-Nai said. "And I'm hungry."

I wiggled my sore feet in my shoes. "Should we go back on the bus?"

I held my breath, waiting for Nai-Nai to protest. But she didn't say anything. I turned, and we walked out of the garden. Before I closed the gate, I looked back at the butterfly garden, and for a moment my heart swelled, so full I thought it might burst out of my chest.

We were quiet on the bus ride back. Four stops to our

corner, and then three. And then we would *finally* go home.

There would be no more scavenger hunts. No clues, no trails through museums, no secret messages at the beach, no more Weiqi games in the park.

And soon, no more May's Bakery.

I leaned my head on Nai-Nai's shoulder. She patted my knee.

Maybe the garden was Ye-Ye's way of saying goodbye to us. *Look*, I could hear him saying. *Don't be so sad, Ruby. Things can still go on. See, look at the wildflowers.*

We lurched back toward Chinatown. Two more stops. The bus slowed, and I felt Nai-Nai getting out of her seat.

"Wait—" I half stood, confused. "We still have two more stops."

"Come on, Ruby. There's a place around here I wanted to show you." Nai-Nai headed toward the door.

I followed her. "Where are we going?"

"There's this place I haven't been to in a while," Nai-Nai said. "We used to go all the time, your ye-ye and I. This ice cream place. Ed's Creamery. It's just around the corner, I think, on Chestnut."

She walked faster. I tried to catch up. We turned the corner.

"They had these fries and these sundaes that they packed so tall you thought they'd fall over. Just wait until you see them—"

And suddenly she stopped.

I looked up. "We're not there yet. This is a shipping store."

She didn't speak for a long time. She stared at the storefront.

"No," she said. "Chestnut and Taylor Street. It has to be here. It *has* to be." Her voice rose.

"Hold on," I said, trying to calm her down. "Here, let me pull up my—" I reached into my backpack and paused, realizing with a renewed sense of alarm that my phone was, in fact, still gone.

And Nai-Nai was no longer calm. "Where is it? Where did it go?"

My eyes flew open. I took a deep breath. "Hold on. I'll go in and ask."

As I stepped in the store, my head raced.

"Hi, what can I help you with? Are you here to ship something?"

"We're looking for an Ed's Creamery," I said, trying to keep my voice from shaking. "Is it . . . around here somewhere?"

She looked confused for a moment. "Creamery?"

I shifted my weight from foot to foot. "Yeah."

She saw my panicked look. "Hold on," she said. "Let me go get my manager."

She went to the back room, and I returned to my racing thoughts.

"I don't know if there's an ice cream place here," she said

when she returned. "My manager says there used to be one, but it got bought out twenty years ago? There's a frozen-yogurt place down the street, if you want."

Oh.

It finally hit me.

Your ye-ye and I used to go here all the time.

There was no Ed's Creamery. There hadn't been for twenty years.

I ran and pushed open the doors to tell Nai-Nai. But she wasn't there anymore. Nai-Nai was *gone.* I turned back to the cashier. "My grandmother," I said. "She was standing right there outside the door. Did you see where she went?"

The cashier stared at me. "Sorry, what?"

"My grandmother," I said, trying to keep my voice steady. "She—" And then without looking back, I dashed for the door and peered outside.

I scanned the ends of the street. There was no sign of her.

I set out on a fast walk, and then started running. I tore through the crowds. I couldn't lose her. I ran to the end of one block, and then another, until I was out of breath and slumped against a building. I searched frantically, craning my neck, for any sign of her. Yellow bag. Floral pants. Gray permed hair.

She wasn't anywhere.

She couldn't be far. Could she have gone north, or south? I looked up at where the sun approximately was.

Where was north or south, even? Would she walk down in the direction of that stop sign, or the other way? I started running in the other direction before coming to a stop. I reached for my phone, and then realized again that I *forgot it on the subway.*

I was alone.

In a city of millions of people.

Outside a shipping store.

And it all hit me at once.

I'd broken the first rule: I'd let Nai-Nai out of my sight, just for that moment. And I'd broken the second: It was late afternoon. Now she was gone.

I was supposed to get her home. But now she was wandering the city. Nai-Nai, who was forgetting names and faces. Who didn't remember that her favorite ice cream shop had been torn down twenty years ago and still talked about going there as if she'd just been there. Nai-Nai, who got lost trying to get to a bus stop.

What if she couldn't find her way home? What if she forgot me?

Why had I let us run away?

Ruby you always cause problems you can't do anything right you—

I paced up and down the street. I passed shops and open stores and afternoon markets. "Excuse me," I said, to people passing by. "Have you seen my grandmother?" Some stared at me blankly. "She's short and wearing flower pants."

They shook their heads, and my heart sank.

What if I had to go to May Wong? Or go home? What if I had to tell Mom and Dad?

It couldn't come to that. I had to find Nai-Nai, even if it meant searching every single street until it got dark. I doubled back, and headed toward where I came from. I passed the park that Ye-Ye and I played Weiqi in.

And then I saw a flash of floral and my heart swelled three sizes.

There she was.

Sitting in that park. Looking up at the trees.

"Nai-Nai!"

I ran up to her.

She turned around and stared at me blankly. "It was just there," she said. "On the corner of that street."

"It's gone, Nai-Nai," I said. "It's been gone for twenty years."

"I saw it," she repeated hoarsely.

I sank into the seat next to her. "I know. But it's gone now."

Nai-Nai looked at her hands. I reached out and hugged her, tightly. I could feel her bony shoulders pressing into my chest. We rocked back and forth.

"It's gone," she said in a small voice. "It's all gone."

I held her tighter. My mouth opened but words failed to form. *I'm sorry*, I said to her, over and over in my head. *I'm sorry.*

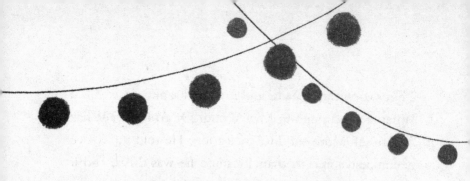

TWENTY-TWO

WE SAT ON that park bench for a while. We watched the pigeons flock to a piece of bread that a kid was throwing. I looked over at Nai-Nai. She stared straight ahead.

"Nai-Nai, we should go home."

"I'm fine," she said.

"I know." I looked in the direction of Nai-Nai's apartment. The afternoon light sloped over the tops of the buildings. "We should still get going. We shouldn't be wandering."

"I'm *fine*," she said. "I see how you're looking at me. I know it's . . . I know it's going. My memory. But I can take care of myself fine," she said, softer. "And I don't want to be in a nursing home."

It was the first time she admitted to what was happening.

"Your ye-ye knew it was going, too," she said. "He would tell me where things were when I forgot. And remind me of names. And to take my medication. He told me to see someone, and I said to wait. Because he was there, and it wasn't so bad. He . . . he kept me rooted."

She looked at me. "But when I lost him, I began to lose a bit of everything, too."

My heart caved in.

"Everything's . . . just out of reach, sometimes." She shook her head. "Sometimes I don't know whether to call you Ruby or Vivian. I can't remember if places are still there or if they're long gone. I thought that when I came back, everything would be just the same as I remembered it. But some days everything is so . . . so different. And now they're going to take me from my home, too."

Her voice trembled. What was it like to live in a hometown that was slipping away from you, the memories fading and the streets changing beneath your feet?

"I'm sorry, Nai-Nai," I said softly. "I'm so sorry. I wish I could have done something that day. I wish—" I stopped. "If only I stayed later. I could have saved him."

She looked at me, her eyes clear. "Don't be sorry, child. Not you. Believe me, I know. I have those thoughts, too. But there was nothing you could have done, I promise."

We sat for a moment more.

"Let's go home, Nai-Nai."

This time, she didn't protest. She nodded, and then

gathered up her bag. But before she stood, she looked over at me. "Thank you for taking care of your lǎo nai-nai this summer."

We stood. We crossed the square, toward the rest of Chinatown. Toward home.

The light cast the city in a golden glow. We quietly walked home, feeling the warmth of the setting sun on our necks along with a cool breeze that had picked up around us. I looped my arm through Nai-Nai's and I wished, suddenly and fiercely and painfully, that there were a hundred more days of summer. That these days would continue and never end.

We headed up the street and toward Nai-Nai's apartment building, finally. But we barely had time to get to the door before someone burst out of it.

I halted. "Liam?"

He stopped himself right before he collided into us and bent over, panting. "You're—here—ohmygodit'syou I just ran down three flights of stairs—"

"Liam, are you all right?" Nai-Nai was alarmed. "Do you need something?"

I asked, "Wait. Why are *you* here?"

Liam sucked in a deep breath and straightened up. "*Everyone's* here." He flung his arms out. "Where have you been all day?"

"Nai-Nai and I were just walking," I said. "Are you okay? What's wrong?"

"A walk??? It's been—" Liam's voice rose in disbelief. "Are you serious? Why weren't you answering any of your calls?"

"I lost my phone! Sorry!"

"We thought *you* were lost!" Liam burst out. People were starting to stare. "We've been looking for you all afternoon! We called and *called* but then we couldn't find you, and no one could, and your parents came and everything and then we all came and then—" He looked at me, and his eyes were wide with alarm. "You need to come upstairs. Everyone thinks you've been missing."

For a moment, the world tilted on its axis, time froze, and I stared at Liam.

Everyone?

"Missing?" Oh, no, no, *no.* "Was this because I didn't answer their texts? I know I was in a hurry and lost my phone on the Muni, I swear—"

"I don't know," Liam rushed on, still out of breath. "They said it was something about your nai-nai missing an appointment. And they kept calling the apartment and then they called you, Ruby, but you weren't picking up—"

I stared at Nai-Nai.

"Ai-yah," she sighed, her shoulders slumping. "Last night they told me they had scheduled a doctor's appointment for this afternoon. I told them I wasn't going."

My jaw practically dropped onto the sidewalk. "And you didn't tell me? *Why didn't you go?*"

"I didn't think they would show up at my door!" Nai-Nai protested. "They never check up on me. I told them no and thought they would just leave me alone like always."

I stopped myself from sinking to the pavement. "Okay. Um. This is really, really bad." I looked up. "Where are they?"

"Upstairs. They're on their way down."

"And how worried are they? On a scale of one to ten?"

"Where does two seconds away from breaking down the door and filing a missing person report fall?" Liam said. "Why on *earth* did you do this?"

I opened my mouth, but Nai-Nai spoke before I could.

"I found out I was going to be put in a senior home today," Nai-Nai said. "So I tried to get me and Ruby to run away."

Liam looked incredulous. "Wait." His eyes widened. "Did you guys—like—you *ran away*?"

"Well, tried. We didn't get very far," Nai-Nai said, smiling a little. "Some might say we walked in a circle."

Liam looked at me.

I didn't know what to say. "Yeah," I said. "I . . ." I paused. "We started retracing the steps. Of my ye-ye's last scavenger hunt." I shook my head. "I thought that maybe—that by retracing his steps somehow, it would help—that it would make everything better." It must have sounded ridiculous. I didn't know how to explain it all to him. That going along on this scavenger hunt was the only way I could think of to calm her down. That we both wanted to search for signs that Ye-Ye had left behind, even though he was gone. And before I knew it, tears sprang to my eyes. "I don't know how that would have made it better, I just—" I threw my hands up, not knowing what to say.

I was going to cry. I hated crying in front of people. I remembered Naomi sitting across from me, looking uncomfortable, not meeting my eyes.

But Liam didn't look away. "Oh," he said. "You went through it all?"

I nodded. "Every stop," I whispered. "I know. It sounds ridiculous."

I bit my tongue and looked at the ground, waiting for Liam to say something. But he didn't say anything. Instead I felt myself being pulled into a hug. "It doesn't," he said. "Trust me, I would have done the exact same."

And then, after a moment, Liam stepped away. "Okay," he said. He looked like he was going to say something else, but he'd hardly opened his mouth before the door burst open again.

"Evelyn! Ruby!" May Wong shouted. She rushed down the stairs and threw her arms around us. From behind her a crowd emerged from the building and gathered on the sidewalk: Auntie Lin. Liam's dad with his nai-nai.

And Mom and Dad.

"Oh, we are so glad you are safe," May Wong sighed.

"We were all worried sick," Liam's dad said.

Dad came forward and folded Nai-Nai into his arms. "Ma, are you all right?" He pulled away from her. "Where were you? What were you thinking, going into the city like that?"

"Ai-yah, I was fine the whole day," Nai-Nai said.

Mom didn't say anything. She just hugged me for a long, long time, squeezing me to her. "I'm glad you and Nai-Nai are safe," she said. She held me extra tight. But she pulled away, and I saw the look on Dad's and her faces, and I knew.

I knew that I was in the absolute, worst trouble of my life.

Everyone lingered in Nai-Nai's apartment for the next hour. May Wong wanted to make food for us, and then we ended up ordering enough Chinese takeout to feed five families. Auntie Lin fussed over us, scooping lo mein into my bowl, and then went home to feed her cats. Liam's dad talked to Mom and Dad for a while, who were helping Nai-Nai get water and talking to her. I hovered around the kitchen table and felt so sick to my stomach I had to sit down. Even Viv came around.

And then, suddenly, everyone was gone.

And it was just Mom and Dad and me and Viv.

Nai-Nai stood from the kitchen table. "I'm going to lie down."

Which left me sitting around Nai-Nai's kitchen table with my parents and sister.

A family meeting, I thought. A family meeting that I

really, especially, did not want to be here for.

Dad took a long sip of water and then set it down.

Mom crossed her arms. "Ruby Chu. What. On earth. Were you thinking?"

"I'm sorry," I said.

Mom's tone was scathing. "*Shǎ yātou.* You just cannot do a single thing with common sense, can you? Not even if we beg you?"

I wanted to shrink until I was invisible.

She stood up. "You just ran off! With your nai-nai! Do you know how dangerous it is to be wandering the city? Did this summer not teach you anything?" Mom yanked out her phone and jabbed it toward me. "Seventy texts, Ruby. I sent you *seventy texts* and called you *ten times!*"

"I'm sorry! I lost my phone on the train!" I burst out. "I didn't mean to, I texted you and then I forgot it on the seat, I *swear.*"

Silence. Viv spoke up. "I've lost my phone on the Muni before," she said, in a low voice. "Happens all the time."

Mom squeezed her eyes shut.

"So if you lost your phone," Dad said quietly, "then *why, Ruby,* would you go wandering with Nai-Nai?"

"That's—" I threw up my hands and tried to keep tears from springing to my eyes. "That's what she wanted to do."

"She had an appointment!" Mom said.

"You didn't tell me about the appointment! She didn't tell me about the appointment! I didn't know!"

"Why do we need to tell you these things?" Dad's face was red. "Why do we need to tell you, over and over again, what is right and what is wrong? You are thirteen, Ruby. You should have kept her home."

"You know how Nai-Nai is," Mom said. "How could you be so—so *irresponsible*?"

"I was trying to bring her home!" I stood from my chair. "The whole day! She was so scared that you were going to come in here and take her to a nursing home that she wanted to *run away*, and I was trying to calm her down so she would go home. Or else she would have run off into the city! Alone!" Tears rose to my eyes. "Don't you *see*? She's scared and she's losing her memory and this whole summer all I've been trying to do is take care of her. I've been helping her remember names and organize her cabinets and helping her walk around and I'm *trying* all I can but I don't know what to do." My voice trembled. "But you can't see that, can you? Because you haven't been around here all this summer, have you? You just shut us out!"

Dad looked up.

"Ruby Chu!" Mom said.

I balled my fists together. And when I spoke, my voice was steady.

"If I didn't tell you, would you have known?" I looked them in the eye. "Would you have known that Nai-Nai was sick?"

Dad opened his mouth and closed it. Mom's knuckles

turned white. Viv looked at me, her eyes wide.

"That's what I thought," I said, my voice breaking. And I turned and walked into the bedroom.

I waited for Mom to raise her voice. I waited for Dad to scold me. I waited for even Viv to say something. But no one said a word. No one came after me, and I knew I was right. But it wasn't a good feeling, knowing that I was right. It felt horrible. We all lived in the same city, but my family had left Nai-Nai behind, by herself, in the middle of an ocean of all her grief and confusion, and that was what hurt the most to realize. I bundled myself in the blankets and pulled them tight around me.

TWENTY-THREE

I COULD HEAR Mom and Dad talking until I nodded to sleep that night. I swore I heard Nai-Nai's voice, too, but that could have been me dreaming. At some point in the night, I woke up when Viv came into the room.

I turned, squinting against the light.

"I'm supposed to sleep here too," she said. "Mom and Dad are taking the couch." She was wearing one of Nai-Nai's big flowery sleep dresses. I moved over. I felt the springs creak under both our weights. I scooted to the edge and faced the window. I waited for her to fall asleep.

But she didn't.

"Ruby?"

I didn't answer.

"I'm sorry Mom and Dad were so hard on you. They shouldn't have yelled at you like that."

I stared at the city lights in the distance out of Nai-Nai's window. But she knew I had heard. And she must have known that I was angry with her, too, because she shifted and didn't say anything else.

I was the first to wake up in the apartment. Viv was still snoring. I padded to the kitchen, to make tea, and then I heard footsteps behind me. "Morning, Nai-Nai."

"Zao," Nai-Nai said quietly. *Morning.* She lifted a finger to her lips, and then pointed at the couch. Mom and Dad were still asleep, with Nai-Nai's crochet blankets draped over them. She stared blankly at her cabinets until I reached in and brought out the jar of green tea. She boiled the water. I spooned the tea leaves into cups. Nai-Nai sipped her scalding-hot tea. I blew on the surface of mine.

Nai-Nai and I drank our tea and looked over at the morning fog. The morning was still ours, after all. I set my cup down and hugged her, tightly.

"Oh, Ruby," Nai-Nai whispered, and I could hear the smile in her voice. She leaned her head on top of mine.

Mom and Dad woke up soon after. Dad busied himself with folding the blanket and putting things in order. He organized Nai-Nai's CD shelf and cleaned up her coffee table. Mom went to wake Viv. And then she came into the kitchen and poured herself a cup of hot water.

"We were thinking," she said softly, not quite looking me in the eye. "Dad is going to stay here with Nai-Nai for a couple days."

"Okay," I said.

"But the rest of us should get home."

"I want to stay."

"Your dad is going to look after her. I promise."

I didn't budge.

"Please, Ruby," Mom said softly. "Let's just go home. At least for today."

Nai-Nai looked at me. "Go on. I'll be all right. Don't worry about me."

I clenched my jaw. "Fine."

I gave Nai-Nai one last hug before I left. Mom and Viv and I took the Muni home in silence. Finally, the exhaustion began to sink in.

"Do we want to make something for breakfast?" Mom said when we got home.

"I can make pancakes for all of us," Viv offered, trying to keep her voice light. For once, she wasn't running out the door to go to brunch with her friends. "How does that sound, Ruby?"

Earlier in the summer, I would have jumped at the opportunity to spend time with Viv. But now I turned away. "You can make it," I said. "I'm not that hungry."

I went upstairs.

I spent most of that day in my room. I reached for my phone before I realized that it was swallowed up by the San Francisco transit system. It was gone for good—I called the support number using Mom's cell phone and got hung up on. I desperately missed having a phone. I wanted to text Liam. I wanted to ask if Nai-Nai was at the senior center, or if she had come back from her appointment yet, or if he knew any news. I guess I could ask Mom to call Dad, but I didn't want to talk to her.

So instead I reorganized things. I cleaned out my drawers. I put all the eraser food and eraser animals back up on my shelf. I put the eraser xiǎolóngbāo that Nai-Nai and I got next to them. I finally dug out the map that I had pushed to the bottom of the drawer. I spread it out over my bed, smoothing out the crinkles. I followed the colorful paths around, like markers of every year.

This map wouldn't change. There would be no new colors, no new routes added. But I took my colored pencils. I laid the map on my desk. And over Fort Mason on the map, I carefully drew flowers.

"The garden is beautiful, Ye-Ye," I said softly. "And Nai-Nai loves it, too." I remembered the rain all winter and wondered if Ye-Ye had been taking care of it, knowing that one day, Nai-Nai and I would make our way to it. That thought made me want to cry all over again.

I heard a knock on my door and jumped. Viv was standing there. "I made lunch," she said. Miraculously, she was still around the house. And she didn't comment on me talking to a map. "Mom wanted me to tell you to come eat."

"Okay."

She glanced at my desk and at the map. I expected Viv to nod and turn away. But instead she came over. She reached out and touched her fingertips to the colored pencil lines. I watched her trace the sky-blue line, the last year she had done the scavenger hunt with us. Viv stared at the map for so long that I wondered if she was trying to figure something out.

"The year with the tide pools," I said. "Remember?"

"Yeah," Viv said faintly. "I remember."

She looked back down. "There are so many lines here." She traced the dark green line, the one that ended at Fort Mason. "And this . . ."

"This was last year."

Viv nodded. "I missed out." She straightened up and started to head out of my room, but not before looking at my shelf of erasers. She looked at them for a long moment. Her lower lip started to tremble, just a bit, and she blinked a lot, and she looked like she was about to say something. But then she walked to the door. "Remember, Ruby. Lunch. Whenever you want it."

I said, "Okay."

My parents went to work. Viv stuck around, peeking in every once in a while. I stayed in my room. Late that Monday night, I heard Dad's car pull into the garage, and then I heard him and Mom talking in their quiet voices. Finally, I couldn't bear it anymore. I crept to the top of the stairs and sat down to listen.

There was a pause. "Ruby?"

Dad stood at the foot of the stairs. I stood up to go back into my room.

"Come join us, please. If you'd like."

I walked down the stairs and sat at the dinner table, my heart hammering in my chest. Viv was already sitting there. In the kitchen light, I could see the lines around Dad's eyes. He ran his fingers through his hair. Mom paused from washing the dishes.

"We took Nai-Nai to an appointment today," he said. He looked straight at me. "We did some cognitive and neurological tests. It's confirmed. Nai-Nai is showing signs of mild dementia, possibly Alzheimer's."

My heart sank, heavy, into my stomach. I knew it. I knew it all along. But still, hearing it was hard. I looked down at my hands.

"We were trying to discuss what to do," Dad said.

I slumped. "So she's going into a nursing home."

"That's . . . one of the options. But she can still take care of herself," Dad said. "So she doesn't need full-time care. Not just yet, while it's early stage. But she does need supervision. We need to observe the progression and alert the doctor if it starts getting noticeably worse."

"I can take care of her," I said.

"No, Ruby," Mom said.

"You can trust me," I said. "I know where everything is."

"Of course we trust you," Dad said. "But we should have never asked you to be the sole caretaker of your nai-nai in the first place. I . . ." He put his face in his hands. "Your mother and I were so caught up in everything this summer that we just . . ." He looked at me. "We should have known this earlier, Ruby. What you and Nai-Nai were going through. I'm sorry."

Mom said softly, "We should have asked."

I stared at my hands.

"I didn't mean to run away with Nai-Nai." Tears smarted in my eyes. "I swear. I was going to bring her home."

"We know," Mom said. She reached out. "It's been a hard year." And this time, she didn't sound judgmental at all. I nodded.

"It has," Dad echoed. "Losing your ye-ye. And everything else."

"I'm sorry if we made it harder," Mom said. "Especially this summer."

I looked up. I didn't want to say *that's okay*, because not everything was okay, not yet, not even close. But at least they were listening. So I just shrugged. "Well, I *am* glad I spent the summer with Nai-Nai. That was nice."

Mom and Dad exchanged a look. "We heard you made lots of friends," Mom said, with a small, tentative smile.

"And one really good friend," I said. One whom I still owed an apology to. "Hanging out with Nai-Nai's friends was nice, too." I looked up. "So if . . . if Nai-Nai gets to stay in her place, can I still spend weekdays there?"

Dad looked at Mom. "We were talking about that, actually," he said. "Another option came up. Since Vivian is moving so soon, she can share a room with you for the next few weeks."

"Why would she be sharing a room?"

Dad looked at me. "We're thinking of having Nai-Nai move in with us. For the time being. How does that sound?"

TWENTY-FOUR

DAD TOOK A few days off work and stayed over at Nai-Nai's, getting everything sorted out. Mom talked about getting me a new phone.

"I can just take Viv's when her old plan expires."

"No," Mom said. "It's about time you got a smartphone of your own. But—" She gave me a pointed look. "*No* losing it on the train again. You hear me?"

"I won't," I said. "Promise."

The days were quieter. It felt strange, not being with Nai-Nai or hanging out at the senior center. I rose early in the mornings and didn't know what to do with myself. But on Thursday I woke up to the sound of honking outside my window. I peered out to see Dad's car coming up the street, tailed by a shiny red car. Dad pulled into the garage, and the car screeched up to the curb.

Dad must be coming back with Nai-Nai. I ran to the front door. "Nai-Nai!"

"Ruby-ah!" I heard Nai-Nai's voice from inside the car. She got out. "I'm here!"

She hugged herself to me and I breathed in the smell of lavender and hundred-flower oil. I glanced toward the shiny red car with the tinted windows. "Who's that?" The car door opened, and out came—

"Auntie Lin?"

She perched her sunglasses on top of her head.

"You—drive *this*?"

"What, you think I spent my entire life working sixty-hour weeks just to retire early with an old beat-up car?"

The passenger door opened and May Wong stepped out. "Ruby," she said, frazzled. "I have something very important to tell you. *Never* ride down hills with Auntie Lin."

"She just doesn't like me driving a hair over the speed limit," Auntie Lin said. "Well, I got here, didn't I?"

"Wait," I said. "Why are you two *here*?"

"We're the Old Lady Moving Crew," Auntie Lin said. "Your nai-nai needed some people to carry some boxes, so here we are." She patted the hood of the car. "Also, I needed to take this one out for a spin."

"Old Lady Moving Crew?"

"Are we not old? And are we not moving things? Speaking of, Ruby, you should stop gawking at my car and go open the door so we can carry things through it."

I hurried to open the door. We spent the morning moving boxes out and into our living room. Nai-Nai's sewing basket and CD collection settled on our dinner table. Nai-Nai was moving into our home, so of course her CDs would have to come with her. Things stacked up in the kitchen. Jars of tea leaves. Nai-Nai's electric kettle.

"We have an electric kettle," I said.

"Mine is faster," Nai-Nai said.

I sighed and draped her crochet blanket over our couch. At some point in the morning, there was a knock on our door. Liam stood outside, grinning. "Hi! I'm here to help move."

"Oh, Liam!" May Wong said. "You're here."

I laughed. "Here to join the Old Lady Moving Crew?"

Liam blinked. "I mean. Yes."

"I recruited him," Auntie Lin yelled from the kitchen. "It's a fiercely competitive process, but he got the role with flying colors."

Liam shrugged nonchalantly. "I'm just that good."

We moved more boxes around and into the kitchen. Dad got us food delivered and went to the store around the corner and bought Liam and me ice cream bars. After every box was put away, Liam got ready to go home for the day.

He turned to me. "Does this mean you and your nai-nai won't be going to the senior center anymore?"

I glanced down. "I don't know. Probably not."

"Don't think this means you're getting rid of us," May

Wong edged in. "Auntie Lin and I promised we were coming over for mah-jongg nights." She turned to Auntie Lin. "*And* we're taking public transit next time."

"Okay," Liam said. "Well, you should come over sometime. To our house. We just unpacked most everything. We even set up the Xbox. You can come play actual games with me and my dad."

"Your maa-maa doesn't play?"

"She reserves the TV for her Chinese dramas," Liam said. "Seven to eight every night. But yeah. You should come. If you want, that is."

"Okay," I said. "I will."

Liam's dad came and picked him up. Mom and Viv went to buy bedsheets for her dorm room, and Dad and Nai-Nai went back to her place to get a couple more things. "My cats need to be fed," Auntie Lin said. "Want a ride back, May?"

"I'll stay behind," May Wong said.

"I'll drive slower this time."

"No, your driving is fine, if not entirely legal," May Wong conceded. "I just wanted to say a few things to Ruby. I'll take the train back."

"Okay," Auntie Lin said. She went to the door, and then paused. And then she came back, rooting around in her handbag. She pressed a handful of Hi-Chews into my hand. "For you," she said. "You missed me winning a lot of bingo this week."

I smiled. "Thanks, Auntie."

There was a slight hint of a smile, and then she hurried on to her car. "Tell Nai-Nai I'll be here for weekly mah-jongg nights," she said. "Don't forget."

And then it was just May Wong and me.

She turned to me. She pulled an apple out of her bag. "Would you like to share it?"

"Okay," I said.

"Come, let's sit."

We sat at the dinner table. May Wong washed the apple, and then began to pare it with a small knife. She cut the apple into four pieces, and then set it between us. I took a piece.

"Ruby," May Wong said. I looked up. "Thank you for taking care of your nai-nai this summer."

I nodded. My stomach twisted into knots. "I'm scared," I said. "I don't know how much she's going to forget. And how quickly. I wish I knew."

May Wong sighed. "I wish I knew, too. I don't know. Our friend Mary held on for a long time. But we all could see what was happening. I'm glad you're there for your nai-nai."

I nodded. We were silent.

"How's the bakery?"

May Wong folded her hands. "We're moving everything out at the end of August." She sighed. "Sixty-three years, and this is how it ends."

"I'm sorry," I said. "For what I said about you. And the bakery. I shouldn't have. It was really mean of me." I took a shaky breath. "I just—"

I'd just wanted things to stay the same. For things to stop shifting and ending. I thought about how May Wong would have to walk to the senior center every week passing the empty walls of the place that had stood for sixty-three years. How I might someday circle back to the bakery, remembering fresh-baked loaves and egg tarts, forgetting, in the moment, that this place had long changed. Which other places like May's Bakery had stood for decades, only to be slowly forgotten by the city? "I didn't want to see it go, that's all. I'm sorry."

May paused for a long moment, carefully watching my expression, before she spoke.

"Let me tell you a story," she said. "When I was in my late twenties, I worked at the bakery. It was the seventies and they were starting to acquire and develop buildings." She sighed. "People got evicted every other day. They tried to fight back and still . . ." She laced her fingers together. "Still many lost their homes." She let out a shaky breath. "Businesses around us were being bought up. My ba thought he was going to have to give up the bakery. It was struggling and . . ." She looked up at me. "Your ye-ye had just come back into the city. He put together a plan to raise money for the bakery. He got us featured in newspapers and got celebrities to come to our place. And it worked. I thought it was going to fold in the fall of 1979. Instead it lasted decades more."

Ye-Ye had never told me that story.

"Every fighting chance I had with the bakery, I gave it," May Wong said. "We've spent years in the red. But these years' debts just keep piling up. It's hard, hard work, running a bakery. It's work we love, but the days and the years really wear on us." She let out a breath. "And when I talked with Annie, she said that she and her family had been thinking about moving out of the state." She looked down. "I knew without a doubt that it was time."

She met my eyes.

"That's why it hurt me so much. Because everything you said, the plan that you and Liam put together, it reminded me of what your ye-ye had done." May Wong's voice was soft. "Only this time, I knew that the bakery had to close." She shook her head. "I'm sorry for losing my temper on you. You have a big heart, Ruby. I know you love the bakery more than anyone. It was always the favorite part of my day, when you came in."

"It was my favorite place in the world," I said. "I'm sorry, May. About the bakery. And everything."

May Wong smiled down at her hands. She pushed the plate of fruit toward me. "Here, eat more."

We were quiet. I crunched into the apple piece.

"Let me know if I can help," I said. "With . . . packing. Anything."

"Actually, I was thinking," she said. "I want to throw one last party for my bakery. Next month, right before we move everything out. And since you're so good with throwing parties . . ." Her eyes twinkled. "Will you help me plan it?"

My heart soared in my chest. "Of course."

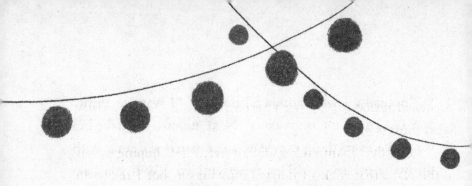

TWENTY-FIVE

"YOU FORGOT THAT one task there," Liam pointed out to me as we played on his Xbox. It was this multiplayer game, where you're stuck in space and you have to follow a map to complete your tasks before time runs out. "Try to get to it by the end of the day, will you?"

"Hey," I said. "It's not fair. I'm just learning and you've been playing it for ages."

"What can I say? I'm a natural," he said.

"More like you've memorized all the maps already."

"That helps."

The moment I'd gotten my new phone, I texted Liam. Turns out, he lived a fifteen-minute walk from my house. I looked around at his living room. Books were stacked haphazardly on shelves. The boxes were in the corner, tucked inside each other like nesting dolls. "You're truly all moved in."

"Finally," Liam said, glancing over. "I'm hoping this is the place that sticks. I don't wanna jinx it, but I really do like San Francisco." He looked over at the dinner plates. "You know my dad finally took holiday decorations out of the box the other day? That's a *huge* sign. Honestly, I might even stay through eighth grade at this rate."

"You have to," I said. "They throw the biggest field day for graduating eighth graders. They set up cotton-candy-making stations and foam jousting."

"I'll try," Liam said. "No promises. But foam jousting seems epic." He put his controller down. "I don't know. We'll see. My dad's still getting his job stuff sorted out." He glanced over. "How is everything going with your nai-nai? We miss you guys at the senior center."

I put the controller down. "She's all right. We're kind of just keeping an eye on her for when she's forgetting things, or stuff like that."

Liam nodded. "And it's good she lives with you now."

"Yeah," I said. I smiled. "So far she's tried twice to get Mom to rearrange the entire spice cabinet. It's kind of funny. But I'm glad she's with us. There's a lot going on in the house, for sure."

"I bet," Liam said. "Viv's going away to college soon, right?"

I nodded. "She's flying out next weekend." Then the weekend after was May's party. And then two more weeks, and then school. This summer really did go by fast.

Liam set down his controller. "I give up on this map," he said. "It's *so* confusing. If I had to design it, I'd make it a lot easier on the players."

"So why don't you?"

"Oh, once I'm done with the class, I will." Liam was taking a two-week online game design class, and he wouldn't stop talking about it. It meant that I didn't see him as much, because I didn't really go to the senior center anymore, and he rarely went. But I'd still see him and his grandmother at Nai-Nai's game nights that she hosted at our house every Saturday.

At one of the first game nights, I'd pulled Liam aside and apologized to him for what I'd said to him the day May told us her bakery was folding for good. But I didn't even get halfway through my apology before he told me that it was okay and that he knew I was hurting inside. I realized then, for the tenth and definitely not the last time, that Liam was probably the nicest kid I'd ever met.

I was lucky he chose to be friends with me.

"I'm bored with this game," Liam said. "Wanna play another?"

I looked toward the rack. "So . . . Mario Kart? It's the only game I'm halfway decent at."

His eyes widened. "You *really* are gonna challenge me in Mario Kart."

I grabbed the disc. "Rainbow Road."

"Seriously, Ruby. You're picking the hardest track? Do you know what you're up against?"

"What, you can't take it?"

"Bring it on."

We flipped through the console. He picked Bowser. I picked Toad.

"Ready?"

"As ever?"

Ten seconds in, Liam hit me with a Green Shell and I fell off the track. "Oh, my God," Liam said sarcastically. "You fell off?"

I turned to glare at him and Toad unceremoniously veered off the track again. I had second thoughts about Liam being the nicest kid I'd ever met. At some point, his dad wandered into the living room. "Wow," he said, peering at the screen. "You're getting lapped, Ruby."

"Hey!" I said, gritting my teeth. "I didn't come here to get roasted by everyone."

Liam's dad joined for the next round. I got lapped by both of them, but I didn't care. Liam walked me through each of the different game maps, and it was then that I got an inkling of something I wanted to do.

"Okay, wait, Liam."

"Okay, wait, Ruby. What?"

"I have an idea."

"And that is . . . ?"

I turned to him. "You know how May Wong is hosting the farewell party for her bakery? Well, I think we could make something for her. Like a gift."

Liam put down his controller. "I'm listening."

And I told him.

The week passed. I hung out at Liam's place a lot. I grabbed ice cream with Viv. Now that she'd temporarily moved into my room, every free inch of space was filled up with all her suitcases. But I didn't mind, because Viv was around and we were talking more.

Mom and Dad made sure to check in on Nai-Nai in the mornings and make dinner for her. Mom was gentler on me. Dad asked how I was doing. I finally told them about what had happened with Naomi and the full truth behind my detention. They didn't get mad. Mom said, "Well, I'm glad you have a really good friend now."

"Me, too," I said. It was time that I realized that my friendships going into eighth grade would look a little different than I thought they would. That Naomi and I might not be close friends, or even friends, anymore. But that was okay.

Mia and I, on the other hand, still called each other. When I finally told her, too, about everything that had happened with Naomi, she confessed to me that Naomi had kind of stopped texting her, too. Mia and I proceeded to FaceTime until it got dark out, just like the old times. I told her about the bakery and Liam. She showed me this gray kitten her family was helping foster and told me she was trying to convince her parents to keep him. Even though we still lived far apart and couldn't talk every day, I knew we'd still be there for each other.

"I might even be coming back to San Francisco sometime in November. To see the grandparents." She glanced at me over the phone screen. "Let's hang out?"

I smiled. "Yeah."

Nai-Nai was quickly taking over the house, filling the tables with new craft projects she was starting up again. Sometimes she shuffled around, confused as to why the walls were different, and I had to remind her that she'd moved out of her apartment. We didn't go to the senior center much anymore, since it was much farther now. Still, Nai-Nai's friends visited us often and came every Saturday night for game night. And with the end of summer approaching, Nai-Nai and I were finally reaching the conclusion of the sixty-episode Chinese drama, claiming the TV every night after dinner. Mom and Dad curiously watched us break down from their places at the dinner table, where they were writing emails. Even Viv peeked in from the pantry, where she was rummaging for dessert.

"Second to last episode," I said, practically jumping in my seat. "They're finally going to talk about their feelings, right?"

Nai-Nai and I clutched each other all throughout the

episode. At the end, the woman was about to go overseas and the man chased her down in the airport to finally confess his love. "We both act for a living," the guy on the screen said softly. "But it was never a show with you. I've known you since we were kids. I've loved you all this time."

Of course, Nai-Nai and I both sobbed into the crochet blanket.

Viv leaned over the couch with a box of cookies. Mom and Dad had stopped writing their emails. I sniffled and glanced back. They all faced the TV, their eyes wide, transfixed by what they saw.

"Wait," Viv said. "The episode just ended like that?"

Dad asked, "What did she say in response?"

"So," Nai-Nai said, turning to me with a twinkle in her eye. "Do we watch the last one?"

"Yes!" Mom blurted out.

I tapped on the screen of my new phone to check the time. It was six thirty on a Saturday. "They're coming over in half an hour for game night," I said.

"Maybe I'll trick them into watching with me instead of playing cards," Nai-Nai said. "Fine. Can we at least *start* the episode?" She turned to my parents. "Come on, watch with us."

We squeezed the five of us onto the couch, and Nai-Nai pressed play.

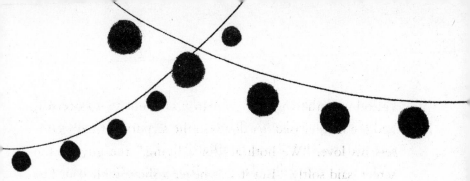

TWENTY-SIX

VIV WAS UP early the Wednesday before she left for college. I was watching the fog roll in outside my window when she tapped me on the shoulder. She was in sweats and a windbreaker, gathering up a sandy tote bag.

"Beach?" I mumbled, half asleep. "Have fun."

"You're coming with," Viv said.

I sat up in bed. "I am?"

"Yeah." Viv looked hopeful. "I mean. If you want. Mom and Dad said I could take you."

"Okay," I said. I pushed the blankets off. "I'll come."

I was still trying to figure out what Viv had up her sleeve and why she wanted me to come when we bundled into the car. Viv switched the radio from NPR to some indie music channel as we drove through Golden Gate Park. We didn't talk much, but the music was nice. Ten minutes later, she parked on the side of the road overlooking a path to the beach.

"Here," she said. She led the way down the rocky path, and then paused. "Look familiar?"

I stopped. I could barely see the Golden Gate Bridge in the distance, its red spires rising out of where the fog met the sea. The waves crashed on the sand, the sea air salty and briny. Near me, pockets of water lapped on the rocks. "The tide pools."

Viv sighed. "Six years ago, remember?"

I nodded. "The fifth stop."

"The last year I came to the scavenger hunts," Viv said, setting down her tote. Her voice sounded a little sad. "I should have come to more. That's what I kept telling myself this year. I wish I had."

"It's okay," I said, trying to make her feel better. "You were busy."

"But I always had a *day*," Viv said. "I mean, out of a whole year, at least I could have spent a day with Ye-Ye. But I didn't even do that."

I was quiet, staring at the cloudy skyline. "We missed you. We even went to look at erasers last year. The ones at the stationery shop you like." I looked at my feet, at the water splashing over the rocks. "I picked one for you."

"Really?"

I nodded. "It was a strawberry cake. With strawberries you could take on and off. It's in my room. I can give it to you. If you want."

"I would love that," Viv said, breaking out into a smile. "I can keep it on my bookshelf in my dorm."

There was a long pause. I pointed at the tide pools at our feet. "Anemone."

She knelt down, peering at the still life in the water. I knelt next to her. For a moment, we didn't say anything. We just peacefully watched the tentacles of the anemone ripple, slowly.

"I heard you visited those same stops this year," Viv said. "With Nai-Nai."

"Yeah," I said. "I think we were both thinking of Ye-Ye. Like we were trying to look for hints of him all over the city. But we didn't really find much. Except for the butterfly garden he left behind."

"A butterfly garden," Viv said, her voice full of wonder.

"It's beautiful, Viv. It's growing really well."

"That doesn't sound like all that bad of a day," Viv said lightly.

"It wasn't," I said. I stared at the surface of the water. My knees were pressing into the rock, so I stood up. "I mean, it wasn't great when I lost my phone and Nai-Nai got confused and wandered off. But it was nice to be with Nai-Nai. I can't really explain it. I know we shouldn't have gone, but I'm glad we did."

"That makes sense," Viv said. She got to her feet. "You know, you were right. We all should have been there more for Nai-Nai." She sighed. "And I should have been there for you, too. Mom and Dad were pretty hard on you this summer."

I shrugged. "I mean, I was kind of the troublemaker kid."

"Yeah, but for valid reasons," Viv said. "I don't know if Mom or Dad remember, but being thirteen *sucks* butt."

I laughed. "Wait, you didn't like being thirteen, either?"

Viv laughed and shook her head. "Nope. I wish I had the guts to ditch school like you did. But it does get better." She brushed a piece of hair from my face. "I just . . . last year was so hard, and being around the house was so hard that I . . ." She shrugged. "I guess my first instinct was just to hang out outside of it. And I kind of spaced myself out from everyone in the family when I should have been spending time with you all before college. I'm sorry."

"That's okay," I said. "You had a lot to deal with, too. Plus, you can always call us."

"Oh, yeah. I'll FaceTime. And if Mom and Dad are being difficult again . . . just let me know. They seem better now, but if you need me, I'm always a call away."

"Promise?"

Viv squeezed my hand. "Promise."

I looked at my feet. "Remember when we 'traveled' to New York?"

Viv looked at me. "Oh, my God, you still remember that?"

I nodded.

"Remember the road trip we were going to take? Across the country?"

"To every state," I laughed.

"We're still going someday," Viv said. She jangled the keys that were looped around her fingers. "Now that I can drive, we can go anywhere."

Suddenly my heart swelled and I threw my arms around Viv. "I'm going to miss you," I said, my voice thick. "I really, really am."

Viv rested her cheek on my shoulder. "I'll call you every week," she said. "I'll be back. Thanksgiving. I promise."

She hugged me back tightly, and we looked at the ocean and at the tide pools some more, watching the fog settle into the sea. Someday, when she came back for her breaks, I would take her to see Ye-Ye's garden. I'd show her the milkweed and the wildflowers and tell her what I learned at the butterfly exhibit, two years ago. That monarch butterflies travel thousands of miles each year, crossing mountains and seas to reach safe land for the winter. But eventually, they come back home. They always know how.

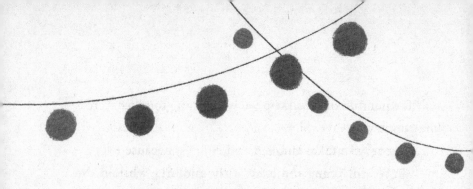

TWENTY-SEVEN

ANY MAY'S BAKERY regular could always tell you that the busiest time of the week was on Saturday mornings. The place always filled up with people who came for the crispy yóutiáo and sugar donuts, especially when a fresh batch came in.

But nothing compared to the night of the goodbye party. Crowds poured out of the tiny bakery and down the block. Hundreds of people responded to the online invite. People took the train into Chinatown from all around the bay. Families bustled in. People in business suits and graying hair wandering up Chinatown poked their heads in to see what it was all about, and then walked out with overflowing boxes of char siu bao. Lights twinkled up on the walls, surrounding pictures taken throughout the years.

Annie ā-yí stood behind the counter, wrapping up buns

and tucking siumai into plastic containers. I caught her eye and gave her a wave. She waved back. The place was filled to the brim with take-out bags and elbows, because everyone wanted to linger and look at the pictures while they snuck a bite out of their coconut bread.

"Look at this place," May Wong said, peering around in wonder. We sat at the table in the corner with Nai-Nai. Mom and Dad were checking out the pictures on the wall.

"It's more crowded than during the Lunar New Year," Nai-Nai said. She had worn a bright white collared shirt and red pants, with red lipstick and gold earrings to match.

Auntie Lin came over with another take-out box full of egg tarts. "Come, eat," she said. "I can't finish these by myself."

"Ai-yah," May Wong said. "The egg tarts are going to run out for the fourth time."

"Well," Auntie Lin said. "Good thing no one knows it was me."

I reached for the egg tart. I offered one to Nai-Nai. "Are you hungry?"

"You know me," Nai-Nai said, biting into the egg tart. I put a sponge cake on her plate while I took an egg tart for myself. I craned my neck to look for Liam.

There he was.

He weaved through the crowd with his behemoth of a computer bag. He reached our table, his eyes lit up. "Okay, so my dad and grandmother are coming in an hour. But

I just passed a bunch of people having a *high school reunion* outside," he said. "Isn't that cool? They all graduated seven years ago but this is the first time they all ran into each other."

"Liam," May Wong said with a puzzled expression. "Are you playing video games at my party?"

"Oh, *this*," he said. He opened his laptop and it screeched to life. "Ruby and I wanted to show you this. It's something we've been working on." He tapped something into his computer and turned it around.

May Wong glanced at the screen. "It's a map."

"An *interactive* map," I said. Ye-Ye's map, with its drawings, had given me the idea. "We put a post on the internet asking for stories from people who remembered the bakery. And if you hover over each dot . . . there's a story."

May Wong's mouth fell open as she leaned in. "But . . . there's so many of them. All over the world."

Liam grinned. "Look," he said. "There's people who live in Chicago and Boston and Canada and even Australia who remember going to the bakery when they were a kid. And it's all *here*. Their stories."

May Wong's eyes became misty. "Oh, I . . ." She couldn't speak for a moment. She shook her head in disbelief. She looked around the table. "Look, Ruby and Liam made *this*."

"We know," Nai-Nai said, grinning. "It was hard to keep it a secret from you."

"These kids are awfully talented, aren't they?" Auntie

Lin mused. She winked at me.

May Wong looked at Liam, and then me. "*Thank* you both," she said. "This . . . this is unbelievable."

"It was all Ruby's idea," Liam said.

"But Liam was the coding whiz," I piped up. "He put it all together."

May Wong called Annie over to pore over the stories on the computer. Auntie Lin went to get another helping of coconut bread.

Nai-Nai stood and wandered over to where Mom and Dad were looking at the pictures. I followed her.

"Look at this," Mom said. In the dim glow of the light, I made out my ye-ye and a toddler with a bowl cut seated on his lap, her lips frosted with coconut flakes.

"Ah." Nai-Nai peered in. "Vivian, that's you."

"That's me," I said. "Ruby."

"Ruby," she corrected herself. "Ruby."

"It was during one of the Lunar New Year celebrations," Dad said. "Nine years ago."

Nai-Nai looked toward the picture in wonder. "Look at Ray," she said. She beamed at us. "I knew he was happiest here."

She squeezed my hand again, and I squeezed back.

I knew that there could be a day where she would look at the picture and not remember who Ye-Ye was. There could be a day where she would look at me and not remember my name, or this night, or the way the place was filled to bursting, with the lights and the laughter. But I would sit down with her and I'd tell her over and over again. I'd tell her about scavenger hunts. I'd sit with her in our house and tell her what I remembered of Ye-Ye.

Nai-Nai started talking about another picture with Mom and Dad. Liam's dad and nai-nai had come in by this point, and Liam's dad started talking to Dad. Mom helped Liam's nai-nai over to the table, and she was wearing the bright finished sweater she'd knitted over the summer.

I stayed in the corner and looked at the picture of Ye-Ye and me, smiling over the desserts. I thought of how much of his life had been here: how hard he'd fought for it to stay open, how he'd reunited with the love of his life here, how he loved the bakery so much that he couldn't even bear to pass this place without stopping by and took me here every chance he got.

And I thought of how many other people loved this place, too.

The walls would stand bare, the shelves gone. The sweet aroma of fresh-baked pastries would dissipate. But tonight, the place was packed full, so full it seemed larger than life. It contained, it seemed, the city. Families from all over. A whole Chinatown showing up for May. A high school reunion just outside the doors.

A group of girls peered into the shop from the street. One of them was buying egg tarts at the counter. She looked up directly at me and I stopped.

Naomi smiled a bit and tentatively waved, as if to say, *Hi.*

Three months ago, I would have run to the street and tried to bring her and her friends in. Now I waved back and stayed where I was. And then, by the time I blinked, they'd passed the shop.

I saw Liam in the doorway, looking out.

I made my way over. Before I reached him, I turned around and took a picture to send to Viv. She spent this week settling into her dorm, but she still called me on Thursday night. "Tell me all about the party," she said.

"I will."

I texted the picture to Viv. Another text came in, from Mia.

Have fun at the closing party tonight! I wish I could be there :) I loved that place and I miss you!

And then she added three pink heart emojis. I sent her a text back, and then tucked my phone away.

And then, finally, I reached Liam.

"Hey," I said.

He looked up at me. "Hey."

"Wanna join us in there?"

He shrugged. "I just wanted to stand outside for a bit."

"Everything okay?"

He looked toward me, and then there was a hint of a smile. "Yeah. I'm fine."

I stood by him. "What's up?"

"It's just—" he sighed. "Sometimes I move into a place

and then after a while I start to think that it's home. I think about starting to like middle school and high school and making friends and keeping them and then every time I *hope* that this is the place, we have to leave." He looked at me. "I don't know. I'm trying to not think about it. Maybe this time will be different. But it's already been a summer, and I can't imagine moving away. It feels like home already. More than Portland. More than anywhere I've ever been in the last few years."

He looked back out at the street.

"I hope you stay, too," I said. "It's going to be your home. I can just feel it."

Liam looked at me, his eyes hopeful. "You think?"

"I know it," I said.

"I hope so," he said. "My dad and maa-maa really like it."

"And we'll always be with you," I said. "Me and my nai-nai. And Auntie Lin. And May." My throat got all tight so I couldn't say what I wanted to next: that he always had a family in us, too. "You know that, right?"

Liam started to smile.

"Come on, last call for egg tarts," I said.

And we headed back in, toward our families and found friends, gathered in the place Ye-Ye and I always called home.

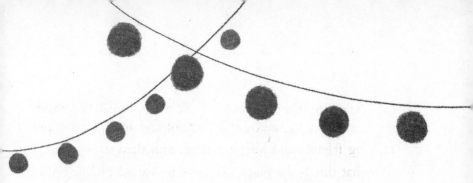

ACKNOWLEDGMENTS

RUBY LOST AND FOUND is such a dear book to my heart, and I owe so much gratitude to those who helped me along the way.

To my agent, Jess Regel, for being such a steady guiding presence—I would be so lost if it weren't for you. Thank you for being the champion of Ruby's story from the start and for never doubting for a second that I could write another book. Thank you for everything, truly, always.

To Alex, for being a dream of an editor to get to work with—your vision and incredible notes always transform my books for the better. To the tireless team at Quill Tree Books: Allison, Rosemary, Mark Rifkin, Laura Harshberger, Robby Imfeld, Emily Mannon, and Kelly Haberstroh. I'm so lucky to be working with you. Thank you so very much. Thank you to the fabulous cover design team: Laura Mock for design and David Curtis for art direction. And to Sian James—thank you for the cover art of my dreams.

None of this would ever be possible without my family. To my wonderful parents—thank you for all those trips into Chinatown, for always relenting to get us treats at the bakery, and for so much more. To Justin—best sibling ever. You're such a star. To my dear, sweet, loving grandparents—I am beyond fortunate to also have been raised by your tender care. I love you so much. This story's for you. To 奶奶 and 外婆，我想你们。To my extended family and my endlessly supportive cousins—thank you for cheering me on all this time and for always eagerly asking for updates at family gatherings. To Yuk 阿姨, for making me feel so welcome on my move, and for the language guidance.

To Katia—I am so grateful for you, dude. I am so lucky to have you in my life. Thank you for everything you've given to me and to Ruby. Thank you for loving her too. To Dave and Paula—thank you for being a second home, for your help with this book, and for everything that you have given me. I love you guys so much, truly.

To more dear friends—I don't know where I would be without you all. To my D.A.C.U loves: Chloe, Racquel, Tashie, Zoe, for the endless laughter and handholding. To my Catan loves: Jake, Joelle, Racquel (again), for making me feel less alone in this industry. To Maeeda, for all the good chats. To Miranda, for your cheerleading and for giving me those wonderful notes. To Grace, for the (now) cross-country friendship. To Karuna, for staying my big sis. To Camryn and Michael, for nearly a decade (whoa) of being friends. To Michelle, for always being there and for the mutual support. To Kamilah, for all of our excited texts. To Francesca, for all our cute SF days and for teaching me about the Muni. To Kalie, for always being in my corner and cheering me on. To Syd, for the lovely text chats. To Birukti, for the check-ins and for the sweetest gift. To Fari—I'm so glad I got to know you. And to Andi, always, for being the reason I am the writer I am today. I owe you so much.

To Gaby, Eghosa, and Cate—love you girls so much (and Cate, thank you for that beautiful spring SF day). To Val, for the tattoo trip. To Lily, for that shared emotional viewing of *The Farewell* in a DC basement theater. To Becca, for being such a big champion of my career. To Katherine, for letting me feature the kitty and for so many other things. To Lauren, likewise, for the pup cameo and, likewise, for so much more. To Jess, for being an endless source of light and warmth. To Rachel and Pranavi, for the standing dinners and for the friendship. To Lexi—I'm so glad we found our way back to each other. To Maeve, for the pen-palmanship. To Jonathan, for helping me out with SF details. And to those who have been so supportive of me: Therese, Nik, Julian, Jake. Thank you.

To Dr. Silvia Russo and Dr. Sharon Sha, for providing invaluable insight into the subjects of dementia and

Alzheimer's, and for adding nuanced knowledge to personal experience.

To Professor Marci Kwon, for teaching that life-changing class.

To the MG #21der crew—we still got each other's backs. Thank you for sticking around and for the continued support. I appreciate you all dearly. To the MG community on the internet—thank you, thank you for being there for me. And to all the kidlit authors I've gotten to meet over the course of my career so far—you are all the kindest people.

To everyone who read and supported my debut novel— a deep, resounding thank-you from the bottom of my heart. To bloggers and reviewers, for your beautiful pictures, your art, your shout-outs, your enthusiastic posts on social media. To all the classrooms I've gotten to visit. To librarians and teachers and educators: Thank you so much. You do tireless work and you deserve the world. And to all my readers—I owe you my deepest gratitude. None of this would be possible without you.

And lastly, to the Chinatowns that have always made me feel at home: Chicago, San Francisco, New York. A specific shout-out to the bakeries. Thank you.